My robot stood perfectly still beside me. I couldn't see through the holes in his mask. His hands, clad in gray work gloves, hung at his sides. I guessed that he was a boy from two clues: he was wearing a spicy fragrance that could only be men's cologne; and his tennis shoes were large.

Mrs. Lanet revealed my robot. "Chad Bennington, take a bow!"

Chad! I turned to look at that famous smile. "We're the lucky two," he said and he winked at me.

"I thought you could only say beep. . . . "

Caprice Romances From Tempo Books

A CAPRICE ROMANCE

T.L.C. Tender Loving Care
Judith Enderle

TEMPO BOOKS, NEW YORK

T.L.C. TENDER LOVING CARE

A Tempo Book / published by arrangement with
the author

PRINTING HISTORY
Tempo Original / October 1984

ISBN: 0-441-80050-5

"Caprice" and the stylized Caprice logo are trademarks
belonging to The Berkley Publishing Group.

Tempo Books are published by The Berkley Publishing Group,
200 Madison Avenue, New York, New York 10016.
Tempo books are registered in the United States Patent Office.
PRINTED IN THE UNITED STATES OF AMERICA

To my husband Dennis
I Love You

⇒§ *One* §⇐

"Benedict, I'm overdue to meet my Prince Charming. Or maybe I should state that differently: My Prince Charming is overdue to meet me. You should go out and grab the next Prince Charming who walks by this house and bring him right to me. Benedict, fetch! Benedict? Do you hear me?"

Benedict, who was a combination sheepdog, standard schnauzer, and who knew what else, yipped in his sleep. But I don't think that was supposed to be an answer to my question. He didn't even hear me. He was too busy dreaming doggie dreams.

I rolled over on my back in the middle of my bed, tucked two navy-blue throw pillows under my head, then painted a mental picture of my Prince Charming on the pale-blue bed canopy overhead. Not surprisingly, he looked quite a bit like Chad Bennington, the president of Patriot High School's student council. Get practical,

Carolyn, I thought. The odds of your dating Chad are about the same as the odds of Benedict dragging him into the yard and dropping him at your feet: zero. Still, dreaming was nice.

But dream time was over. This was supposed to be study time, and my schoolbooks were scattered at the bottom of my bed. I sat up and reached for *Modern Calculus*, changed my mind, and decided to start work on an English composition. I wished that the only homework I had was for art class. That wasn't drudgery, like these other courses. Art was satisfying and fun.

There was a quick tap on my bedroom door, then my friend Brita burst in. "Hi, Carolyn. No one answered my knock at the front door, so I let myself in," she explained.

It wasn't worth explaining to Brita that she moved too quickly for anyone to answer her knock. Like a ray of sunshine, Brita Hodges dazzled everyone. She was energy in motion, whereas I was a silent observer. We were opposites in other ways, too. Brita was little, blond, involved in everything. And me? Medium all over, with brown hair, and involved only in art.

She landed on my bed with a bounce, which sent my mattress into spasms and caused *Modern Calculus* to slide off the edge and land in front of Benedict. He looked up to see who had invaded his territory, sniffed the book, then rolled onto his side to continue his nap.

"Carolyn, wait 'til you hear. I just came from the student council meeting. Our special project, the one that will leave our mark on Patriot High, is going to be fabulous. No other class has done anything like this. It will make that little mosaic the class of eighty did look like nothing. This idea is absolutely super!'' Brita bubbled with enthusiasm. All the while she talked, her hands moved and her blue eyes sparkled with excitement. ''Best of all, you're going to be in on it.''

''Me?'' Warning flags went up in my head. Brita's goal in life was to get me involved in one of her projects, and I didn't want to be involved. ''Brita, you know I have to study. Good grades will cinch my acceptance to the university, and they don't come easily for me the way they do for you. Please, don't volunteer me for anything.'' I tried to go back to the first sentence of my composition, that introductory sentence that was always so difficult to get right.

''Put your books down for a minute. Five minutes won't make a difference in your grades, Carolyn Dawson. Listen to me.''

I sighed. Brita got excited over everything—the first school dance, the first school play, the first football game; the last spring sale, the last day of school, the last one to finish a race—who was usually her boyfriend Fred. ''All right. Tell me about this never-to-be-equaled project.''

''All right. You know when you go into school there are the two halls that go right and left inside the doors? To the right is the gym and to the left is the principal's office and then the counselors' offices.''

''As I recall, the school does look something like that. After almost four years there, I'm vaguely familiar with the layout.''

Brita exhaled with exasperation. ''Carolyn, if

you weren't my absolute best friend and if I didn't know that you'll be just as wild about this idea— once you hear it—as I am, I'd forget about telling you."

"Brita, just tell me."

"I'm trying. Anyway there's a long wall between Mr. Olston's office and the counselors' offices—blank space. Our project is to paint a mural on that wall and—the best part is coming; this is where you fit in—the art department will supervise the work. Isn't that great?"

"Wait a minute. What kind of mural?"

"That's the next-best part." Brita pulled her legs up and crossed them Indian-style. "We're going to have a competition. Anyone can submit a sketch to be considered for the mural. We're going to give a savings bond for the best sketch idea submitted. All we have to do is raise money for the prize and the supplies and have the contest. Chad is working on that part. He usually has great fundraising ideas. Doesn't that sound terrific?"

Anything involving Chad Bennington sounded terrific to me. But a chance to win a bond sounded great, too. Ideas started to form in my mind. "That does sound great," I agreed.

"I knew you'd think so." Brita slipped off my bed. "I have to get home. I couldn't wait to tell you about this. Start thinking about a mural right away."

"Aren't you going to submit an idea?"

"I'm student council treasurer and will be busy enough. Anyway, student council members aren't eligible to compete. And besides, my creative talents lie someplace else. Just ask Fred." She giggled and opened my bedroom door. "See you in school tomorrow, Carolyn."

"What do you think about that, Benedict?" I asked when she was gone.

My dog got up, stretched, and yawned—much like a person, which I often thought he was, as did he . . . maybe a Prince Charming under the spell of a wicked witch. But I'd tried kissing him and nothing had happened except that he'd kissed me back, rather sloppily. Now he woofed a short, deep bark, which meant "feed me."

"All right, you big puppy. Don't give me any ideas for the mural. I'll find one by myself." My idea had to be one that represented the students of Patriot High, the city of Charleston, and the state of South Carolina. I'd have to put my creative artist's thinking cap on. Benedict and I headed for the kitchen.

"Was that Brita who was here?" Aunt Elise's whole body shook as she mixed biscuits in a bowl. She stopped, wiped her hands on her bright-yellow apron, tucked a strand of smooth white hair into the coil at the back of her head, then reached for the flour canister.

"It was Brita. She came to tell me about the student council meeting. Come on, Benedict. Let's get your bowl." I went out back with Benedict following me.

"I do wish she'd ring or knock," Aunt Elise said, half to herself but loud enough for me to hear.

Aunt Elise is Daddy's sister. She's lived with us for eight years, ever since Mom died. But I didn't feel especially close to her. I don't know if that was because she wasn't my mother, or because she always seemed to be so set in her ways. I felt as if she disapproved of me and my friends, even when she didn't say anything. Aunt Elise and I didn't talk very often or very well together.

I picked up Benedict's dish from outside the back door and went inside to fill it. He had to eat in the yard because he was so sloppy. But he never seemed to mind outdoor dining as long as he was fed.

While Benedict was eating, I set the table for our dinner, then returned to my room to finish my homework. But instead of English and calculus, I found myself thinking about ideas for the mural. Magnolias, thirteen colonies, patriots, textiles, tobacco . . . and there was so much history to consider! I had a lot to choose from.

When Daddy called his familiar "The captain's home. Where are you all?" I dropped everything and raced to greet him. He caught me in a hug, rubbing his bristly face against mine.

"Daddy, you need a shave," I said.

"But I shaved last week, magnolia blossom," he replied.

"Magnolia blossom" was his pet name for me. Sometimes I thought it sounded silly or childish, but most of the time I didn't mind.

"Something smells good, Elise," he called.

"Dinner will be ready in fifteen minutes, Tom." My dad and Aunt Elise always said the same thing, too.

When we were all seated at the table, I told them about the contest for the mural and the need to raise money for the prize and the supplies.

"You are going to enter, aren't you?" my father asked.

"Of course, Daddy. I have to think of a prize-winning idea."

"I'm sure you will, dear," said Aunt Elise. She passed the crab casserole.

"Maybe the art class could have an art sale to help raise money," my father suggested.

"I'll mention that to Brita. If I could win the bond, it would be a nice addition to my college fund."

"Are you still planning to study art, dear?" Aunt Elise blotted her mouth with her napkin.

I nodded because my mouth was full.

"I wonder if that's practical. Shouldn't you consider teaching or nursing instead? Tom, what do you think? Carolyn would make a good nurse."

Why did she have to bring this up at the table? I wondered. Wasn't it up to me to decide what I wanted to study?

"Elise, I didn't know you had anything against the arts," said my father. "If I remember correctly, you always loved to dance and you sketched some rather beautiful drawings when we were in school."

I looked from my father to my aunt. Aunt Elise knew how to draw? Why hadn't anyone told me? "Do you still have your drawings?" I asked. I didn't know much about my aunt or her life before she came to live with us, I realized.

"No, Carolyn, dear. I haven't thought of them in years. I suppose your grandmother threw them out when she moved into her apartment." Aunt Elise stood up. "I'll serve dessert now if you're both ready. Tom, would you care for iced coffee? I believe we're going to have an early summer."

"The temperature is warm for April. High humidity does that. I thought I smelled rain," said my father. "Iced coffee would be fine, Elise," he added, noticing that my aunt was still waiting for an answer to her question.

While I helped clear the table after dinner and rinsed the dishes before putting them in the dishwasher, I thought about the mural. If only I could win! I was sure I had a chance. *Patriots* is a key word, I thought. They would represent everything. I'd have to get out my reference books and see which men were considered patriots. One I knew was Colonel Isaac Hayne, who was imprisoned in the Old Exchange and executed without a trial. But there were others. I'd simply forgotten them. I'd definitely include patriots.

In my bedroom, the open windows let in the evening spring breeze. My lacy priscillas danced on the windowsills. Thunder rumbled in the distance. I guessed my father was right about rain. Like a sailor, he knew the weather and did a good job of predicting. And like a sailor, he loved the water. That was why he called himself captain. I think it was his dream to own a sailboat. I knew that when he wasn't teaching at the medical university, he was over at Charleston Harbor, sometimes watching and sometimes with his friends who did have boats.

Picking up my sketch pad, I made notes about my first mural idea. Maybe it wasn't the one I'd go with, but it was a start. Brita had been right. This was an exciting project, much better than that little mosaic in the front walk done by the class of 1980. While I worked, I pictured myself winning the best mural idea contest and Chad Bennington presenting me with the prize.

Outside Benedict howled as thunder rumbled closer. Then I heard the patter of drops on the bushes outside my window and smelled the moist, earthy scent of spring rain. Jumping up, I went to rescue my dog. He followed me back to my room, wagging his tail gratefully, then stretched out on his rug beside my bed, while I went back to work.

As I leafed through my old history books, looking for information and ideas, I wondered about Aunt Elise. What kind of mural would she design, if she were going to enter this contest? Maybe I'd ask her. Had she taken art classes in school? And what about dance? There was a lot I didn't know about my aunt, such a private person. I wondered if she'd ever tell me anything about herself.

❧ *Two* ❧

The next morning, the sidewalks were still damp from the heavy rainstorm. I turned up the walk to school, skirted a couple of puddles, and glanced at the round mosaic set in the concrete just below the steps. Years from now students would climb these same steps and inside they'd see our mural. And who knew where we'd be? It was both scary and exciting to think about.

I felt energetic this morning as I jogged up the steps then pushed through the front door. A quick glance to the left showed the long blank wall awaiting the gift from this year's class—a magnificent mural designed by the gifted and talented art student, Carolyn Dawson. I smiled at how egotistical I could be inside my head where no one else could hear or know. Several students called hello as I walked down the hall toward the rows of gray metal lockers. I waved and went on to my locker, where I sorted out my books, then continued on to find Brita.

I spotted my friend outside the library talking with Chad. My heart seemed to beat in double thumps when I saw him. It wasn't that he was incredibly handsome. He was of average height, not more than a few inches taller than I. His hair was dark-brown and straight. His brown eyes were rather ordinary and topped with thick, dark eyebrows, and his nose was a little too large. But he had a wonderful smile, which he directed toward me now. And his friendliness! He had a way of making everyone feel special, even students like myself whom he barely knew.

"Hi, Carolyn," he said. "Brita says you're busy at work with a mural idea. Good luck."

"Thanks." I felt like a grinning clown and couldn't think of a thing to say other than that one word.

"I'm going to discuss my idea with Mr. Olston. If he gives the go-ahead, I'll let you know, Brita," he said.

"He can't help but say yes." Brita smiled and wrinkled her freckled nose.

"I wouldn't bet on that," replied Chad. "I'll see you both later." He walked off, stopping along the hall to talk with almost everyone, it seemed.

"Are you working on a good idea for the mural?" Brita asked.

"You told Chad I was, didn't you?"

"I want him to notice you." Brita smiled. "Did I lie?"

"No, you didn't lie." I tried to stay calm and not blush. Brita's plots wouldn't help. Chad Bennington was too busy to notice me. And besides, he could have any girl at Patriot High; why would he choose me? "I started right after you left yesterday," I said. "Oh, and I told my aunt and my dad about this project. My dad suggested that we could have an art sale to raise money."

Brita nodded and looked thoughtful. "That would probably bring in some money, if the adults in the community were in the mood to buy art; but the student council wants this to be a school project entirely. Anyway, Chad has come up with a fabulous idea. Walk with me to my locker, and I'll tell you about it. Mr. Olston has to say yes."

We started down the hall, retracing the way I'd come. Brita kept her voice low as we went. "Don't breathe a word of this until Chad gets the okay. Then we'll make the announcement. Here's what he wants to do. Oh, it's so exciting, Carolyn." Even with a soft, low voice, Brita exuded enthusiasm. "We're going to have a robot raffle. Doesn't that sound great?"

"A robot raffle?" I frowned at the picture that came to mind. "I guess. Where will we get a robot? And what would you do with it if you won? I think my dad's art idea—"

Brita laughed and grabbed my arm. "Not a real robot, Carolyn. There will be a dozen robot students. If you win one, the robot will be yours to do whatever you command for a whole day."

"Oh," I said. I was glad Chad wasn't there to hear how stupid I'd been.

We reached Brita's locker. Quickly she took out her books for class, then slammed the door shut.

The noise didn't make a dent in the normal before-school commotion that was building to a crescendo in the halls.

"Let's look at the bulletin board. I want to see if there are any summer job notices posted yet," she said. "I'd like to work as a tour guide this year, either on the horse-drawn carriages or maybe at the Old Exchange. Don't you love the dungeon underneath? I sometimes imagine what it would have been like to be a prisoner there."

"I try not to imagine what it was like. The dungeon gives me the creeps." My neck and arms prickled just thinking about it.

Brita and I were so different, yet we'd been best friends all through high school.

She laughed. "Anyway, isn't Chad's idea great? We can agree on that."

"It's different," I said.

While we were looking at the bulletin board—which contained scholarship information, navy recruiting information, and almost every kind of information except about summer jobs—Chad came out of Mr. Olston's office. He leaped in the air shaking both fists above his head when he saw us. Obviously, Mr. Olston had been in a cooperative mood. "Good news! He gave us the green light. We'll make the announcement later today. Start recruiting, Brita. Do you want to be a robot?"

"I'm treasurer. That's enough," said Brita. "Carolyn, how about you? Will you be a robot?"

"No, Brita. I'm not robot material." I shook my head.

"Oh, come on. It will be fun."

"You have fun your way; I'll have fun mine."

"Sign her up to sell tickets," Chad suggested. "I have to find Fred and Toni. They haven't even heard the plan."

"Fred is home with the flu," said Brita. "I'll call him after school. I think Toni is studying in the library. I saw her go in earlier."

"I'll try and catch up with her before the bell rings. See you later." He started away, then turned back. "We'll have a quick meeting during lunch hour," he called.

"All right."

Then Chad was gone, jogging down the hall.

"Are you sure you won't be a robot?" asked Brita.

"I'm sure. Everyone will want to win the popular kids. Someone would feel bad if they won me."

For a minute Brita stared at me with her mouth open. "That's the dumbest thing I've ever heard you say, Carolyn Dawson. Anyone would be glad to win you. You're certainly not unpopular. Sometimes I could shake you. You need more self-confidence. Stop worrying about what people think. Besides, if you're a robot, no one will know who you are."

"I know they won't. Because I'm not that popular."

"Aargh." Brita growled at me and shook her head. "Are you purposely acting dense or what? No one will know who you are because you'll be wearing a robot costume."

"Chad didn't say anything about costumes."

"He doesn't know. I just thought of them. If all

the robots are disguised, no one will know which robot he or she has won until the raffle is all over. The suspense will be terrific. I can just see how it will all work."

"Is this going to be a drawing or an auction?"

"Drawing. I think more kids will buy a chance. Some of the shy kids would be afraid to bid in an auction, but they might buy a book of tickets."

That was me, I thought.

"So will you please be a robot?" Brita's eyes looked pleading. "For a best friend?"

"No, Brita. I really don't want to. But I'll sell tickets as Chad suggested."

"All right. I guess that will have to do." Brita sighed. "I wonder if Fred will be a robot."

"If you ask him, he will," I said.

"I have to have influence with someone," she retorted.

The bell rang and the halls filled with students heading toward classes.

"Everyone will know by next week who the robots are," I told her as we walked toward class. "No one can keep a secret in this school."

"We will this time." Brita stopped outside the computer lab. "And you will be number one on the list for selling tickets. You'd better sell a lot."

"I'll sell my share," I said, and turned toward Calculus class.

The hours passed. When would everyone hear about Chad's idea? I wondered.

It was almost the end of fifth period when the crackle of the PA signaled that an announcement was imminent. Chad's friendly voice came over the mike. "Hello, fans out there in school land.

How are classes going today?"

You could hear the groans and boos that issued from the classrooms up and down the hall. I was in English class and Mrs. Lyndeworth, the teacher, shook her head and raised both hands in front of her for silence.

"I'm going to cheer you up even more," continued Chad. "Mr. Olston has given me this time for a very special announcement; so listen carefully. This year's student council is sponsoring the first robot raffle. Every one of you lucky, lucky students will have the opportunity to win your very own robot for a day. The more chances you buy, the more chances you have to win one of a dozen darling, decidedly dexterous robots, stalwart volunteers from our Patriot High senior class. The money earned from this unique raffle will go toward another project just as unique. This year's graduating class wants to leave behind a special remembrance."

"Chad Bennington," said someone in back of the room.

Laughter rippled through the class.

"Shsh," Mrs. Lyndeworth said.

"We are planning to paint a mural on the long wall between Mr. Olston's office and the counselors' offices. Funds raised from our raffle will go toward paint supplies. But more important, the raffle will also fund the purchase of a United States savings bond, the prize for the most original idea for the mural. You don't have to be an art student to win. Just draw your idea in whatever way you can. It's the idea that counts. The teachers and PTA officers will be the judges. Our art department will do the sketching and supervise the actual painting of the mural. So remember, robot raffle and mural contest. Further details on tickets for the raffle and when the mural ideas are due will be forthcoming. Keep tuned to this station. Chad Bennington, your student council president, signing off. Thank you, Mr. Olston."

Mr. Olston came on the PA, saying that he hoped everyone would support the student council projects. Now we could go back to work.

The classroom buzzed with comments after the announcement.

"I could sure use a robot to write my English composition," said Jerry Leonard, who sat behind me.

"I could use one to paint our house. That's my dad's latest project. Two stories and guess who gets to do the second floor," Brad Holdrick moaned.

"I'd love my very own robot," said Milly Eastman. "Do you think Donny Forbes will be a robot?"

"Don't count on it," Becka Lawry replied. "He's captain of the basketball team. He doesn't have time to be a robot."

"Boy, it sure would be neat to win him." Milly sighed.

"But I do wonder who will be robots," Becka said. "If it's someone I want to win, I'll buy a million tickets."

"If you could afford a million tickets, Becka, you could buy a real robot," said Jerry.

"Class, let's have a little order," Mrs. Lyndeworth said. "We don't have time to read compositions now. Pass your papers forward, please. Tomorrow's assignment will be to write a composition entitled 'Why I Want to Win a Robot.' " She smiled while everyone groaned.

I closed my notebook and slipped my pencil into my purse. What if you didn't want to win a robot? I wondered. I wouldn't know what to do with one if I did win. If I'd been Jerry, I'd have raised my hand and asked Mrs. Lyndeworth. I'd have to make up something, I decided.

Brita and Chad would be glad to hear how popular their idea was. I'd stick to working on the mural. I really wanted to win that bond.

❧ *Three* ❧

After changing out of my school clothes and into my old jeans and a cool shirt, I picked up the work I'd been doing on my mural idea and went in search of Aunt Elise. I found her in my dad's study. She was sitting in his old brown leather wing chair with her feet propped on the footstool. She was reading the current issue of *Better Homes and Gardens*.

"Aunt Elise?" I stood in the doorway, hesitant to intrude upon her.

"Is there a problem, Carolyn?"

"No. Not really." Guiltily I realized that the only time I sought my aunt out was when I did have a problem that I couldn't solve on my own. Otherwise she was just there cooking, cleaning, doing the laundry. Studying her while I stood in the doorway, I noticed that although her hair was almost white, her face wasn't very lined. She was my father's older sister, but she wasn't really that old. I entered the room and sat down on the foot-stool.

"I wondered if you would help me with this idea for the mural," I began. "I've decided that patriots are important because they represent the school name and Charleston, but I'm not sure how I want to put my ideas together."

"Do the rules of the contest allow help?" asked Aunt Elise.

"I'm not sure," I replied. "I'll call Brita and ask."

The phone was on the old rolltop desk which always stood open. I punched the buttons and hoped that Brita was home. Behind me I could hear the crackle of magazine pages turning.

"Hello." The friendly voice of Mrs. Hodges came clearly across the wires.

"Hello, Mrs. Hodges. This is Carolyn. Is Brita home yet?"

"She just walked in two minutes ago. I think she's sampling pecan brownies. One moment and I'll tell her you're calling." The receiver clunked, and I could hear Mrs. Hodges calling Brita. "She'll be right here, Carolyn," Mrs. Hodges said a minute later.

"Um, good. There. I'm finished eating."

I could picture Brita licking crumbs from her fingers before she picked up the phone. Then I heard the scrape of the receiver as she lifted it from the table.

"Hi, Carolyn. Did you change your mind about being a robot?"

"You never give up. No, I didn't change my mind. By the way, your idea went over big in

English comp. class. I think it's going to be a great success. Even Mrs. Lyndeworth picked up on the idea." I told her about our assignment.

"It wasn't my idea. It was Chad's idea. The feedback we got was good, too. So, what's up?"

"What are the rules for the mural contest? Can family members help?"

For a minute Brita didn't answer. "Well," she finally said, "we haven't worked all that out just yet. But I'd say that you could have some help, but the main work has to come from the student. So you could discuss your ideas and rough them out with your family, but the final sketch would have to come from you and the main idea would have to be yours. We'll have to work that out at our meeting tomorrow. The thing we don't want is some kid turning in an idea done by a commercial artist. It should come from the students. Does that answer your question?"

"I think so. Is the contest for seniors only?"

"We had a big argument about that. What we finally decided was that since the effort is being sponsored by the student council, which represents everyone, not just the senior class, everyone is eligible. But the work on the mural will be done by the senior class and the raffle will be run just by the senior class. Anything else?"

"How's Fred? Is he going to be a robot?"

"Fred is feeling better. He'll be back to school tomorrow. And I can't tell you if he's going to be a robot. Robot identities are secret."

"You won't even tell me? Your best friend?"

"I won't even tell my mother. Not even the other robots will know who they are. It's top secret. Don't try to pry it out of me."

"All right. When is the raffle?"

"In about two weeks. Chad will make another announcement tomorrow. There is one other way you could help, Carolyn. Would you make a few posters to put up around school about the raffle?"

"Sure. I could do that. Thanks for the information, Brita. I'll see you tomorrow."

"If you have the posters finished tonight, bring them right to the library in the morning. The student council officers will be meeting in the A/V room."

"I'll do my best." I hung up and turned to Aunt Elise. "You can help, but I have to do the majority of the project. We have to hurry. We have less than two weeks."

She closed her magazine. "Let me see your work so far."

"I've made lists. Before I do any sketching, I want to have an idea firmly in my mind."

"Then let's look at your lists," she said.

I showed her my list of representative ideas and my list of patriots.

"But what about school?" she asked.

"The school is named Patriot High."

"Yes, dear. But this seems somewhat one-sided. Too much patriot. Shouldn't you include books, students in caps and gowns, and learning, which can be represented in many different ways? And what about friendships?"

"I see what you mean." I made notes on another sheet of paper. "Maybe I have to divide my mural into sections and make each section represent the things you mentioned. Then I can decide how to blend the sections together.''

"That sounds like a good place to begin,'' said Aunt Elise.

"Thank you,'' I said.

She smiled, and I noticed that she had blue eyes the color of forget-me-nots. My dad had blue eyes, too, but his tended more to a gray-blue. I had brown eyes like my mom. I remembered her telling me when I was very little that she had Indian blood and that's why she had brown eyes. I don't know if it was true or not. I hadn't thought about that in a long time.

My aunt picked up her magazine again, while I straightened my mural papers into a neat pile. "Aunt Elise, did you take any art classes in college?'' I asked. "Or dance?''

She folded her hands on top of her unopened magazine and sighed. "I wasn't ever able to attend college.'' Her voice sounded sad and her eyes had a faraway look. "And I know you'll think this sounds hypocritical after what I said last night, but I did want to go to college and if I'd gone I'd have majored in art—not teaching or nursing.''

"But why didn't you go?'' I asked.

"Your grandfather wasn't well. You never got a chance to know him. In fact he died a couple of years after I graduated from high school. But it was his dream to see that his sons got a college diploma. He wouldn't count on your father or our brother Joseph getting scholarships. He said it was necessary to have money ready. So I had to go to work to earn money for my brothers.''

"But that wasn't fair. Couldn't my dad and Uncle Joe earn their own money?''

"Oh, they did. Some. But your grandfather didn't want them to work too much. They had to study—a lot."

"I still don't think you should have had to help them."

"My dear, only recently has equality made the headlines. Traditionally, men have always been considered more important. They were the bread-winners. They were the military. If I were your age today, things might have been very different. Although I can't be sure. Your grandfather was stubborn and opinionated."

"But Grandma is stubborn, too."

"I think she had to be to survive living with your grandfather. I don't want you to think that he didn't love us. He did in his own way, although loving fathers were only starting to come into vogue then."

"Well, I guess you helped. Because my dad went to college and so did Uncle Joe."

Aunt Elise nodded. "Yes, they did."

"Then why didn't you go after they graduated? Why don't you go now? Now you can study anything you want."

For a minute my aunt stared at me. "Go to college now?" She sounded surprised by the idea. "But I'm over fifty years old, child. It's been years since I was in school."

"Brita's mother goes to school."

"It's close to thirty-five years since I've had to study for an exam. I don't know if I could." She sounded doubtful, but there was a sparkle in her eyes that made me go on.

"I know you could. You'd only have to take

one or two classes at first, Aunt Elise. We could go together!''

Aunt Elise laughed. ''No, Carolyn. I don't think so.'' She put the magazine aside. ''Let me see your mural idea when you have a rough sketch. You do some interesting things in school these days. When I was in high school, students were seen but not often heard. And we had a lot more homework.''

''Now you sound like Daddy,'' I said.

''And speaking of your father, I'd better get the chicken started. He'll be home before we know it.''

''Think about college, Aunt Elise,'' I said. ''Today women can even be astronauts.''

''Astronauts! I think the correct term for that would be 'far-out'?'' She laughed and shook her head then hurried out of the study.

I carried my papers to my room and spread them out on the drawing table in the corner. Benedict came padding in. I guessed that Aunt Elise may have thrown him out of the kitchen. He was a terrible beggar when food was being prepared. And because he was so big, he could easily reach the counters and the table. I smiled as I remembered the coconut cake that had disappeared right before my father's birthday last year. We'd never found a trace of it. Aunt Elise hadn't even had a chance to frost it.

I bent down and gave Benedict a big hug. ''You're such a nice old doggy,'' I said.

He wagged his tail and nuzzled me for more attention. Absentmindedly I scratched his ears while I thought about Aunt Elise. I was beginning to feel as if I knew her better. And it still made me angry to think that she'd wanted to go to school but had had to work to pay for her brothers' tuition. "That was definitely not fair, Benedict," I said.

Benedict looked at me with sad eyes. He pushed at my arm with his cold nose to remind me that I'd stopped scratching his ears. "I have to do some work, puppy," I said, giving his ears and head one more good rub. "Go lie on your rug."

Obediently, Benedict padded to the dark-blue oval throw rug and stretched out.

I taped three sheets of art paper together to give myself lots of working space. With a light pencil I marked the left side *Patriots,* the middle *Friends,* and the right side *Learning.* I worked for about half an hour before I heard the front door open and close.

"The captain's home. Where are you all?"

"It's past your dinnertime, Benedict," I said. "Why didn't you tell me?"

I raced into the hall with the dog behind me. "I forgot to feed Benedict," I said, stopping to give my father a quick kiss and hug.

"Hurry up before he tries to eat me," my father replied.

I laughed. The idea of gentle Benedict eating anyone was ridiculous.

"Dinner smells good, Elise," he called.

She gave her usual answer.

During dinner I brought my dad up-to-date on the mural contest and the robot raffle.

"We could use a robot around here. Your aunt would have a list of things he could do. Or is a robot a she?"

"I think it depends on which one you win," I said.

"I'm not fussy. When the tickets go on sale, I'll take two books—one for me and one for your aunt."

"Thanks, Daddy. Do you think anyone at the medical school would like to buy a ticket?"

"I'll take a book and ask," he said.

After dinner I returned to my room. I replaced my mural work with four sheets of posterboard and set to work on some advertising for the raffle. I found that I enjoyed drawing some very original robots. I hoped that Chad would like my work when I took it to school in the morning.

⋅§ *Four* ҉⋅

The next morning I arrived at school earlier than usual. I carried the four posters I'd drawn, holding them carefully so they wouldn't bend and wrinkle.

After a brief stop at my locker to leave my books, I headed toward the library. I stopped at the door. My insides felt shaky, the way they did before I had to get up in front of a class to give a speech. *Why am I so nervous?* I wondered. *The posters are good. And I know everyone who will be at the meeting.*

"Good morning, Carolyn."

What had felt shaky grew to a repeat of the great Charleston earthquake as I turned around to look right into Chad Bennington's brown eyes.

"Let me hold the door for you," he said. "I'm eager to see what you have there. Brita promised to talk you into some super promotion work."

"I only had time to finish four posters last night." I even sounded nervous.

"Four! I'd have been happy with one or two. You must have worked half the night, Carolyn."

"Until a little past midnight," I said. "After the first one, the others came easily."

"That's the way it is with most things." He smiled and winked at me. Could he see how scared I was?

We walked down the long aisle between library tables toward the room in the back. Beyond the glass partitions, I could see Brita and Fred waiting for us. Again, Chad held the door for me. I walked past him and put the posters on the table.

"Oh, Carolyn, this top one is great," said Brita. "Chad, do we have to wait for Toni before we look at these?"

"I'm here." Toni, out of breath from running, reached the door before Chad closed it. She was very tiny, even smaller than Brita, with waist-length black hair. She reminded me of the girls on Hawaiian travel posters, although I knew she was Vietnamese. "Oh," she said softly as she stepped up beside me to look. "Beautiful. You drew these, Carolyn?"

I nodded.

"Doesn't this robot look like Mr. Olston?" Fred pulled his glasses down on his nose, puffed out his cheeks, and twiddled a pencil between his fingers, a good impression of our principal.

"He does not." I looked at the round-eyed robot on the first poster. "He doesn't have glasses on." I had tucked some pencils behind his nut-and-bolt ears, though.

"That's all right, Carolyn, we won't tell," teased Chad.

"What do the other posters look like?" Toni asked.

Brita and Fred moved the top poster aside.

"Ah. Mrs. Lyndeworth." Fred frowned, pulled his blond hair down on his forehead, and waved his hands up and down.

"Fred," I began. "What if the teachers think I drew cartoons of them?"

"Quit teasing Carolyn," said Brita, smoothing his hair back in place. "Anyone can see that's me." She frowned and waved her hands up and down in front of her.

"Actually the next one is you—and Fred," I said, moving the second poster to reveal a drawing of a pair of robots fancifully named Raffles and Ruffles.

"Did she draw my beauty mark?" asked Fred, pretending to scrutinize the poster very closely. "Whew. Thanks, Carolyn. I wouldn't want anyone to know—except Brita." He winked and Brita punched him.

"You two quit the clowning," Chad said. "These are terrific, Carolyn. What does the last one look like?"

The last poster showed a robot mowing a lawn, while in the background a kid rested in a hammock.

"That's what I'd do with my robot if I won one," said Toni.

"But we aren't eligible to play, are we?" asked Fred.

"Sure you are. Mr. Olston will handle the ticket stubs," Chad told him. "If you buy the tickets, you have a chance." He turned to me. "Carolyn, thanks again. We'll put these posters up during lunch hour. Now, I hate to throw you out, but we have to discuss some of the details of our raffle, and they're highly secret. Sorry."

"That's all right," I said.

"I'll see you at lunch," said Brita.

"Are you going to enter the mural contest?" asked Toni, as I opened the door.

"I'm working on it already," I said.

"I can't wait to see your entry," she said.

Toni and Chad sat down at the table as I closed the door. All of them looked very serious as they began their meeting, but I couldn't hear what they were saying. I glanced back once at Chad. He had turned a chair around and was straddling it. Leaning forward, he talked, counting off something with his fingers. I sighed. I wished he saw me the same way I saw him. I didn't think he dated anyone special, but he always had someone with him at the dances and games. Who wouldn't want to go out with Chad Bennington? I thought. I knew I would, but he'd never asked.

After that Thursday morning, all anyone talked about was the robot raffle. I worked intensely, trying to get my mural idea ready. Bed never came before midnight; my wastebasket overflowed with discarded beginnings; but at last I completed an idea I thought was perfect and a winner. When I'd finished the final draft, Aunt Elise approved and even said maybe she was wrong not to encourage me to major in art. When I hugged her, I thought I saw tears in her eyes.

My posters hung in the school halls, and competition was strong between classes to sell the most tickets. Mr. Olston had offered a half-day picnic on the schoolgrounds for the winning class. You couldn't go anywhere without someone asking if you wanted to buy a ticket.

The two weeks were almost gone. With my father's help, I'd sold more than my share of tickets. Aunt Elise had bought two books just for herself. She said she had all kinds of odd jobs she could use help with.

Brita was running constantly, counting money, keeping track of the daily ticket stub returns. Mr. Van Lawrence, the art teacher, was in charge of the mural contest submissions. He would only say he was proud of the work he'd seen from his students. He wasn't one of the judges, however. He felt he might be biased.

And throughout all this, no one knew who the twelve robots were.

I was coming out of Calculus class when Brita grabbed my arm. "I'm glad I saw you, Carolyn. I'm going to be kind of glad when the raffle is over. Chad really started something with this idea. No one expected it to be this big. We'll have enough money to buy something for the school as well as do the mural. Do you know we had to print more tickets?"

"That's great," I said.

"But there's one problem."

"No, I won't."

She looked puzzled. "No, you won't what?"

"No, I won't be a robot."

"Oh, Carolyn. That's all taken care of."

"Then maybe," I said.

"Don't be so suspicious."

"You want something."

Brita grinned. "Yeah. I do. How many tickets did you buy?"

"I sold ten books."

"That isn't what I asked. How many did you *buy*?"

"My family?"

"No. You."

"None."

"Not even one?"

"Brita, I wouldn't know what to do with a robot if I won one."

"Aunt Elise would know, wouldn't she?"

"Sure. She even has a list in case. She bought two books of tickets herself."

"Then if you win, you could give the robot to your aunt."

"I suppose."

"Good. Buy my last two tickets. Please?"

"But why?"

"Why? Because I want to sell them. Because I can't buy them. I'm flat broke. I spent all my money on tickets."

I opened my purse. "Doesn't Fred want to buy them?"

"He's broke, too. You don't know how committed this student council is."

"Isn't ten books commitment enough?"

"For friendship's sake," Brita pleaded. "I'll never forget this."

"All right. You twisted my arm. Just put your name on them."

"Uh-uh. You paid for them. You get them."

"That seems silly. With two tickets against my aunt's two books and probably other people's dozens, I won't win, anyway." I handed her two dollars, and she gave me the receipts.

"Thanks, Carolyn. You're a true friend. And you've saved my reputation as student council treasurer. Can you imagine what would happen if I had to turn in unsold tickets tomorrow morning? Total embarrassment! One more day! This is so exciting! I can't wait."

I smiled. Brita was bubbling again. I didn't care about the raffle, but I couldn't wait to find out who had been chosen to win the bond and have their mural painted.

"I probably won't see you until assembly tomorrow. There are a lot of details to take care of tonight and in the morning. Thanks again and good luck," she called as she ran off down the hall.

The auditorium was packed with laughing, talking kids. Everyone was saying what they'd do with their very own robot if they won.

Jerry Leonard and some of his friends were walking stiff-legged up and down the aisle, stopping whenever they saw a pretty girl to say, "Give me a kiss, cute unit," as if they were robots.

I tried to tell who was missing from the audience. I didn't see Fred or Chad or Brita or Toni, but they had to be onstage anyway, or someplace behind the curtains, to help with the raffle. Finally I sat back and gave up. There was no way to tell who was here, who was absent, or where anyone in particular was sitting with all the bedlam going on.

But when Mr. Olston stepped on the stage, there was almost immediate silence. Looking down the rows, you could see students holding on to handfuls of ticket receipts.

"Students of Patriot High," Mr. Olston said, beginning this assembly the same way he did all the others, "please rise for the pledge of allegiance to the flag of our great country."

Seats squeaked and feet shuffled as the student body stood up. Then all those voices that had earlier created such a cacophony blended to speak in one voice. ". . . and justice for all." More squeaking of chairs, a few whistles and clapping, then Mr. Olston went on.

"This has been one of the most successful fund-raising efforts to take place in recent years here at Patriot High. I'd like to call Chadwick Bennington, president of the student council, to the podium to say a few words."

"Oh, Chadwick. Where are you?" called someone.

More whistles as Chad walked across the stage and raised the microphone just a notch.

"It isn't I who should get the thanks, Mr. Olston," he said. "I take credit for the idea, but the kids were the ones who sold those tickets and submitted their entries for the mural. We should say thanks to everyone for doing their part. Patriot High will never forget this fund-raiser. Not only did we hit our goal for supplies and the bond, but we made enough to present a check to the library for the purchase of new books, each to bear a bookplate showing that that book came from the students. Great selling!''

The auditorium echoed with cheers and stamping feet, as Mr. Cooper, the librarian, walked on-stage to accept the check.

When the noise quieted down, Chad added, ''Now, Mr. Olston's secretary, and a friend to every student at Patriot High, Mrs. Lanet, will announce the winner of the mural contest.''

Clapping and whistles greeted Mrs. Lanet, a slender blond lady, as she walked up to the podium.

''Thank you all,'' she said softly.

More whistles and cheers.

I crossed all my fingers and even my toes as best I could.

''There were so many marvelous entries. We're going to display them in the art room all next week for you to see. But a winner has been chosen. The bond for the mural goes to Derrick Jones. Will Derrick come to the stage, please?''

Who? That wasn't my name. I opened my eyes. Until the minute she said Derrick, I hadn't realized that I'd closed them. Tears of disappointment welled up inside, but I refused to allow any drops to escape. I'd really wanted to win that contest. I'd worked so hard on my entry.

''Derrick's entry will be posted on the wall where the mural will be painted. Take a look. We felt it was very representative of the spirit of Patriot High. Thank you.''

Derrick followed her off the stage, clutching an envelope. Derrick Jones, I thought. He was a sophomore, and he didn't even take art.

"Now for the part of the program you've all been waiting for." I looked up at the sound of Brita's voice. "Our janitor, Mr. Dolby, will draw the twelve winning numbers. If you have one of these numbers, please stand. Toni Mai, student council vice-president, will escort you to the stage to stand by your very own robot." She spun a huge drum packed full of ticket stubs.

Mr. Dolby wore a blue suit. Under the stage lights, his bald head looked polished. He reached into the drum. After digging deep, he handed one slip of paper to Brita.

"First robot goes to number one-ninety-four."

There was a silence for a minute. Then a scream. "Me! My cousin won!" Someone I didn't know—I thought she was a junior—jumped up.

At the same time, the curtain on the stage parted. Standing in two rows of six were identically dressed robots. Except for height and the numbers one through twelve pinned to their chests, there was no way to tell who was who. Each robot wore gray sweats, gray cotton work gloves, and a silver paper bag with holes cut for eyes, nose, and mouth. They stood perfectly still.

Toni escorted the excited girl to the stage where she stood beside robot number one.

"Junior Mary Jo Cleveland is our first winner," said Brita. "Or rather, Mary Jo's cousin Perry is." All of Mary Jo's friends clapped.

The next number was drawn and the next. Each was greeted by excitement, then the winner was escorted to the stage. Mr. Olston won robot number ten, which made the robot stagger slightly, and everyone laughed. Gradually I was caught up in the fun and excitement of the drawing. There were only two more tickets to draw. I hoped Aunt Elise would win. I knew she'd be as disappointed as I was that I hadn't won the mural contest.

⋙ *Five* ⋘

"Two more lucky winners to go," said Brita.

Mr. Dolby spun the drum then dug into the middle of the slips of paper.

"Robot number eleven goes to ticket holder number five eighty-three."

I looked around, waiting for the excited winner to jump up.

"Check those stubs," Brita said. "Number five eighty-three."

I leafed through the pile of tickets in my hand. Then I froze. One of the last tickets—one of the two I'd bought from Brita—was number five eighty-three.

"You must be out there," said Brita. "Five eighty-three?"

Timidly I raised my hand.

"Here," said the girl behind me.

"There," called the boy across the aisle.

Toni came up the aisle to get me. I felt as if I had puppet legs when I stood up and had to grab the back of the seat in front of me for a minute.

"Congratulations," said Toni.

I smiled, because whatever words were inside my head couldn't find their way to my mouth. Then she was leading me down the aisle. I could feel all the eyes watching me as I climbed the steps at the side of the stage.

"Our eleventh winner is Carolyn Dawson," Brita said. "Okay. One more ticket, one more robot."

"Stand beside number eleven. You'll know who your robot is in a few minutes," Toni told me.

I don't want to know. I don't want a robot. I want to get off this stage where everyone is looking at me and sit out there where no one notices me, I thought. Obediently, I stood where Toni had told me to go.

I glanced at the tennis shoes my robot wore. They were old and one had a rip in the side. Why didn't I pay more attention to tennis shoes? I wondered. But you don't want to know who the robot is, I argued with myself.

Everyone was clapping. I stopped talking to myself and looked up to see Milly Eastman running up the steps. She was jumping up and down with excitement.

"That's it. Thanks, everyone, for selling those tickets. Now, Mr. Olston has a few things to say to everyone." Brita stepped aside.

Mr. Olston left his place next to his robot and came to the microphone. "First, let me assure you that this raffle was not rigged. My wife is the winner, and she'll be delighted.

"There are some rules the robots and their winners must agree to follow.

"Robots cannot be asked to do anything illegal, immoral, or dangerous."

"Aww," someone groaned.

The audience laughed.

When they were quiet again, Mr. Olston continued. "Robots must cooperate to the best of their ability for a period of one day commencing at eight o'clock tomorrow morning and ending at six tomorrow evening.

"Robots may only speak when spoken to, and their vocabulary will consist of only two phrases. 'Beep,' which will signify agreement or understanding or any other phrase of accord. 'Does not compute,' which will mean that your robot is saying no or that he does not understand.

"Chadwick Bennington will say a few last words before you're dismissed back to class. First, however, with those few rules for robot management outlined, we'll have the great unmasking of the Patriot High robot team. My secretary will do the unveiling honors, while Brita Hodges makes the introductions. One robot at a time, please, Mrs. Lanet."

My robot stood perfectly still beside me. I couldn't see through the holes in his mask. His hands, clad in gray work gloves, hung at his sides. I guessed that he was a boy from two clues: he was wearing a spicy fragrance that could only be men's cologne; and his tennis shoes were large.

Brita was at the microphone again so that Mr. Olston could stand beside his robot.

Mrs. Lanet removed the paper-bag mask from the first robot.

"Heather Trainor, take a bow," said Brita.

One by one Mrs. Lanet revealed each robot's identity. Mr. Olston's robot was Fred Greely, Brita's boyfriend. She clapped the loudest of all, and everyone laughed at the expression on Fred's face.

Then Mrs. Lanet reached me. What would I say to a robot I didn't want? I'd give him to Aunt Elise. I hoped it wasn't anyone I knew well. I tried to think of how I'd explain.

"Chad Bennington, take a bow," Brita was saying.

Chad? I turned to look at that famous smile. "We're the lucky two," he said and winked at me.

"I thought you could only say beep," I answered, surprising myself.

Chad laughed.

The assembly was over, and all the robots and winners went backstage. I gave Chad my phone number and address. "Will nine-thirty be all right? We don't get up before eight on Saturday morning."

"Beep," Chad said. "I learn fast," he added when I laughed. "I'll see you tomorrow."

During afternoon classes, various kids stopped to congratulate me and to tell me how lucky I was. Most of my classes went by in a blur. I expected to wake up any minute and find out I was dreaming. But the dismissal bell rang, and I was walking outside, another week of school ended, and tomorrow was robot day.

"Carolyn, wait!" Brita ran across the lawn to meet me. "Congratulations," she said, for what must have been the zillionth time.

"Brita, thanks, but I think he should have been yours. It was your ticket."

"Uh-uh. You bought the ticket. You won fair and square. And you wouldn't want to disappoint Chad. Think of your robot's feelings. He'd have to go through life as the rejected robot."

"All right. Enough," I said.

"Besides, are you going to tell me, cross your heart and don't tell lies, that you don't want him?"

I glanced away from her teasing eyes, but knew I was blushing.

"Come on, Carolyn. I've seen you looking at Chad. He's a great guy. Besides, it's only for one day. And you can share him with Aunt Elise. Watch him charm her."

"Brita, I never know what to say to him. I know he's nice, but my tongue gets tied up in knots when he's around."

"Oh. It's like that," Brita said, nodding.

"Like what? I'm not good at talking to boys, that's all."

"You talk to Fred all right."

"Poor Fred," I said. "He has to work at the Olstons'."

"Never mind changing the subject, my friend. Fred will survive. Actually he and Mr. Olston get along quite well. We were discussing you and Chad."

"There is no me and Chad."

"But you'd like there to be."

"I never said that."

"You didn't have to. Your face says it for you. And I've suspected as much."

"You didn't rig—I mean, you didn't—"

"Don't even think such a thing. The drawing was completely fair. Haven't you ever heard of fate? You were meant to win Chad. The forces that arrange such things guided Mr. Dolby's hand. By the way, did you give him your address and phone number?"

"Why would Mr. Dolby want my address and phone number?"

"Ah, you're becoming quick of wit and sharp of tongue. That's what winning a robot will do for you. Not Mr. Dolby. Chad. Did you give him your address and phone number?"

"Of course."

"Then, as the French say, let nature take its course."

"When do the French say that?"

"I don't really know if it's the French. And maybe they say it when they're planting gardens. Anyone can say it when the time is right. And the time is right now for you and Chad."

"But . . ."

"No buts. Enjoy. I think the French say that, too." She looked up at the honk of a horn. "There's Fred. Do you want a ride home?"

"I guess, if he doesn't mind."

"Of course he doesn't mind. Come on."

"It's the lucky lady," said Fred when I slid into the backseat of the old Volvo. "And Chad's the lucky guy. Congratulations, Carolyn."

"Thanks, Fred. Why does everyone congratulate me? I didn't do anything."

"Sure you did," said Brita. "You won Chad Bennington."

Fred spun the car into a U-turn. "Brita, why couldn't you have won me?"

"I thought I already had," she said, reaching up to pat his face.

"Well then, what are you doing tomorrow?"

"Helping my mother. Robots aren't allowed to recruit outside assistance."

"No one said that onstage."

"It's an unwritten rule of the robot."

"And how would you know?"

"Never mind. I just do."

"And she claims to love me. I hope you'll treat your robot with TLC, Carolyn," said Fred.

"TLC. That's tender, loving Carolyn." Brita giggled, while I stared out the window so Fred wouldn't glance in the mirror and see that I was blushing.

"All out for the Dawson plantation," said Fred, as he stopped the car in front of my house. "Just remember that slavery has been abolished."

"You'd better hope Mr. Olston remembers. Thanks for the ride, Fred. I'll talk to you tomorrow, Brita."

"You can count on it. I'll call you if you don't call me." She was grinning as if she'd won someone herself. "Say hello to Aunt Elise for me. Sometimes I think she doesn't know who I am."

"Oh, she knows." I shut the car door. "She can tell by the way you run in and out of the house."

"But—"

I smiled and waved as Fred pulled the car away from the curb. I'd finally left my friend speechless.

"Aunt Elise, I'm home." I dropped my books on the floor inside the door and stooped to greet Benedict, who'd answered my call. "Hi, puppy. How was your day today? Were you a good dog?"

Benedict wagged his tail and the rest of him, then tried to give me a king-sized doggie kiss, which I almost managed to avoid.

"I thought I heard you call. Well?" Aunt Elise held garden gloves in one hand and her trowel in the other. "Benedict and I were having a discussion about whether or not he could learn to dig weeds. We were on our way to find out, when he turned tail and ran. For a minute I thought he'd understood every word I said."

"He might have." I laughed.

"The news must be good. You're absolutely sparkling, dear. Come in the kitchen. I'll pour some lemonade."

"The news is good but not good," I said. My new relationship with Aunt Elise made me happy. I was sorry I hadn't talked with her more often and sooner. Brita would probably say live and learn. She and Aunt Elise both liked sayings.

"Tell me the whole story." She also seemed more relaxed lately.

"We didn't win the mural contest, Aunt Elise. A sophomore named Derrick Jones won. They're going to hang his entry in the school hall. I'll let you know what it looks like."

"Oh, dear. I'm sorry. I was sure . . ." She

sighed. "That just goes to show, you can't count your chickens or your awards. But didn't you say there was some good news?"

I nodded and sipped my lemonade. "I—we won a robot."

"A robot! We did? Did my ticket win?"

"Mine."

"Then you must decide what to do with him, her . . . it?"

I smiled. "Him. His name is Chad Bennington."

"Chad. What a nice name. Is he a nice boy?"

"Very nice." The kitchen suddenly seemed warm.

"I see. When is our robot Chad coming?"

"I said nine-thirty tomorrow morning. I hope that's not too early."

"Not at all. You'll have to get busy with a list of chores. Would you like a cookie to go with that lemonade, dear? I made some sugar bars this morning."

"Just one," I said.

Benedict came from under the table and whined.

Aunt Elise broke a cookie in half and gave him part.

"I didn't know that you understood Benedict," I said.

"We have some very long conversations when you're at school, my dear. I'm surprised he didn't tell you. But then, I'm not always sure he understands me."

I stared at Aunt Elise. Was this the same aunt who always seemed to keep to herself? Who always acted so proper? Maybe she'd been like this all along, and I'd just never noticed.

"Don't look so shocked, Carolyn. Do you know that after we had that talk about college the other day and about being old, I took a good look at myself—something I've been avoiding for a number of years—and I realized that I was getting to be an old fuddy-duddy in some ways. Benedict had been trying to tell me, but I didn't listen to him, of course. So, I want you to help me put a stop to creeping fuddy-duddiness. If I start to nit-pick, you may tell me. Don't tell your father that I've said so, though. He'll tell me all the time."

I laughed. I liked this Aunt Elise.

"What do you think about dying my hair?" she asked.

"Oh, I don't know. Your hair is pretty the way it is. Maybe one step at a time," I said.

"I suppose you're right. Fuddy-duddy isn't really an external characteristic. It's mostly on the inside."

I swallowed a laugh at the face she made, still not sure if I should laugh at my own aunt.

"Maybe I'll get my hair cut first." Aunt Elise stood up. "I have to get to the gardening. That's one thing you can put on your list for the robot—weeds. Another thing: Benedict could use a bath."

Benedict rolled over and pretended to play dead.

"He understands every word you say, Aunt Elise," I said.

"Then he'll have to understand that playing opossum won't do a bit of good. He still needs a bath," she replied.

I wondered if Chad was ready for an assignment like that. Well, he was my robot, and he had to do anything reasonable. Did bathing Benedict come under that heading, though? I wasn't sure Chad would think so. I knew Benedict didn't.

❦ Six ❧

I never get up before eight on Saturday. So why was I awake at seven? Chad. That was why, though I blushed when I admitted it to myself. Why hadn't I told him to come at eight? I wondered. I gave up a whole hour and a half I could have spent with him. With my hands behind my head, I dreamed marvelous possibilities for today. Could a robot be ordered to kiss his mistress? I wondered.

With that thought, I jumped out of bed. You're getting carried away, Carolyn. For someone who can barely talk when Chad Bennington is around, you have some outrageous ideas.

I spent the next hour getting ready. After a scented bath, I chose my pink cotton pants and a matching pink blouse to wear.

"Interesting dog-washing outfit you're wearing this morning." Aunt Elise peered at me over the morning paper. She was still in her cotton robe and floppy slippers. Her hair was braided down her back.

"I'm not washing the dog. Chad is," I said.

"I see," replied Aunt Elise. "Who's going to hold Benedict?"

For a minute I simply stared at her. Then I looked down at my pink outfit, so crisp and pretty. I sighed. "I'll change into my jeans and a sweat shirt after breakfast."

"I'm not criticizing," she said. "Simply being practical. Sometimes it's necessary, you know."

"Mm-hm." I poured a glass of orange juice and took a sip. My appetite wasn't there this morning. Excitement had taken its place.

"Where's Daddy?"

"Gone sailing with a friend from the university. He told us, but I don't think you heard much last night."

I reached for a slice of toast and didn't answer. Would my father be home in time to meet Chad? I wondered. I hoped so, though I wasn't sure why.

After clearing the dishes from the table, I ran to change my clothes again. My jeans had patched knees and the sweat shirt I pulled on had once been navy-blue but was now a faded shadow of its former self. This outfit wouldn't make Chad notice me, that was for sure. Practicality could be a real pain.

The sound of a car door slamming sent me to the window. Chad was coming up the front walk. He also wore old jeans and a gray sweat shirt. I still had to brush my hair and teeth and put on lipstick.

Benedict barked when the bell rang.

"I'll get it," called Aunt Elise.

I hoped she'd changed out of her robe. It seemed so important to make the right impression on Chad.

"You must be our robot," I heard Aunt Elise say. "Carolyn will be right down. Won't you come into the kitchen and have a cup of coffee?"

"Beep," Chad replied.

I covered my mouth to stifle the giggle that tried to escape.

"I assume that means yes," said Aunt Elise.

A few minutes later I entered the kitchen. Chad held a coffee cup in his right hand; with his left he was scratching Benedict behind the ears.

I needn't have worried about Aunt Elise. She'd changed into a skirt and blouse. She looked as crisp and efficient as ever.

"Hi. I guess you've met my Aunt Elise?" I said.

"Beep. Beep," said Chad.

I turned to Aunt Elise. "He's only allowed to say 'beep' for yes or agreement and 'does not compute' for no or I don't understand."

"I'd guessed as much," replied Aunt Elise.

"Chad, are you ready to go to work?" I asked.

"Beep," said Chad.

"I made a list. I thought we'd start with Benedict." I pointed to the dog.

Chad looked at Benedict, too. "Does not compute."

"I've said that about Benedict myself," said Aunt Elise. "Excuse me. I'll clear this table and make my shopping list. When you're finished with the dog, Carolyn, I'd like the robot to go shopping for me, please."

"All right, Aunt Elise. We'd better get busy, then. When I said we'd start with Benedict, Chad, I meant he was first on the list. He needs a bath."

What Chad couldn't say in words, he said with his facial expression. His eyes were wide and his eyebrows raised in exaggerated surprise. He looked at me, then at Benedict, whose ears went down, then back at me.

"I'll help," I said.

"Beep, beep," replied Chad, as if saying, "Thank goodness."

"Come on, Benedict." I snapped my fingers at the dog.

Benedict crept under the table, so that I had to get down on my hands and knees and reach for his collar, then drag him out.

"We'll get him outside first, then I'll get a bucket of warm water and the other dog-washing equipment. Chad, you'll have to hold on to his leash, otherwise he'll run behind the hedge and be very hard to get out." I snapped the leash to Benedict's collar.

Immediately, Benedict became a limp dog.

"Benedict, come on. Get up. Heel," I ordered.

Benedict rolled over.

"I'll pull. You push, Chad," I said.

"Beep."

"I'll bribe." Aunt Elise took a cookie from the cookie jar and went to the back door. "Here, Benedict," she called.

Benedict rolled upright and lifted his head to sniff.

I pulled. Chad pushed. We slid him toward the door.

Finally he gave up and got up to reach for the cookie, and we shoved him out the door.

"Beep, beep," said Chad, wiping sweat from his forehead.

"You can say that again. I'll be right back with all the dog-bathing equipment," I said. "Don't let him leave. Hold on tight to the leash."

Chad sat down and petted Benedict.

I didn't think he'd have any problem keeping my dog there. Quickly I gathered the necessities for Benedict's bath. Inside, I filled the bucket with warm water, then stretched the hose in the sun, so when we rinsed his coat that water would be warm, too—at least at first.

"I'll hold Benedict. You wash him," I said.

Chad started by emptying half the bucket over Benedict, who promptly shook half the bucket back at both of us. "Beep, beep, beep," said Chad.

"That's supposed to mean yes," I teased.

He grinned, doused Benedict with shampoo, and scrubbed.

Benedict tried to leave, and I braced my heels on the cement patio to keep him there.

Chad added more water; and Benedict promptly shook himself again, sending soap everywhere, so that it looked like a freak snowstorm had hit our yard. Chad was undaunted. He scrubbed some more, then turned the hose on Benedict to wash the bubbles away.

Chad rinsed while Benedict shook. We all got soaked, but finally, Benedict was clean.

Taking an old towel, Chad rubbed Benedict's fur partially dry.

"Beep?" he asked, which I interpreted to mean, "Is that enough?"

"That's fine." I turned Benedict loose, and he promptly rolled around in the grass.

"Does not compute. Does not compute. Does not compute!" shouted Chad.

Benedict stopped. He tipped his head to one side and barked before he began running, charging from one end of the yard and sliding to a stop at the other, then racing off again in wider and wider circles.

"The bath made him feel like a puppy again," I said.

"Beep." Chad laughed at Benedict's antics.

"Oh, my. You two are soaked." Aunt Elise poked her head around the edge of the door. "Maybe if you sit in the sun you'll dry off. I'll bring a snack. Do robots eat cookies?"

"Beep, beep, beep." Chad grinned. "Beep," he said again.

"I think they do, Aunt Elise."

We dragged two chairs and a small table from the shade to the sun. It was almost eleven o'clock. Washing Benedict had been a full-scale project. I dropped into one of the chairs and tilted my face to the sun. The warmth felt good. Beside me, Chad stretched his legs out. His jeans were dripping with water.

"Did you bring extra clothes?" I asked.

"Beep," said Chad.

"Why don't you go get them? You'll catch pneu— No, I take that back. You'll get rusty. You got the worst of Benedict's bath."

"Beep," Chad agreed. He jumped up and went

around the side of the house. He closed the gate before Benedict could follow him out of the yard. A few minutes later he was back with another pair of old jeans.

"Use the bath by the back door," I said.

I thought how comfortable I was with Chad today, not at all as shy as I usually was. Why wasn't I tongue-tied any longer? Was it because I was in control of the robot? Or was it because the robot couldn't talk back? Whatever the reason, I was having a good time, so far.

Chad returned carrying a tray of cookies and lemonade.

"Thank you," I said.

"Beep." He placed the tray on the table.

"After you've refueled," I said, "we have to go to the grocery store and then the flower garden has to be weeded. I'll watch this time."

"Does not compute," he said.

"Grocery shopping?"

"Does not compute."

"Weeds?"

"Beep."

"You don't know how to weed?"

He pulled two blades of grass. He held up one. "Beep?" he said. Then he held up the other. "Beep?" he said again. "Does not compute?"

"This is like charades. Are you saying you aren't sure which are weeds and which are flowers?"

"Beep," he said.

"Likely excuse. I'll supervise, then. But first I'm going to change my clothes and get the grocery list from Aunt Elise."

"Beep." He held out the plate of cookies.

"Thank you, robot," I said as I took one.

"Beep," he said again.

As I walked toward the house, Benedict went to mooch cookies from Chad. One thing about my dog, he didn't hold a grudge, no matter who gave him a bath. Also, he'd do anything for a cookie.

I put on another pair of jeans and a yellow T-top. I looked longingly at my pink outfit. Maybe another time I'd be able to wear it for Chad, but it wasn't suitable for weeding the garden, either. I stopped still, holding my hairbrush in midair. Another time? Why did I think there would be another time? I wouldn't win him again. Today he was mine, but only today. Prince Charming exists only in fairy tales, Carolyn. Don't expect too much. But standing in my room brushing my hair was wasting the precious time I did have with Chad Bennington. I finished my hair and hurried to the study where Aunt Elise was working on some embroidery.

"We're ready to go to the store, Aunt Elise," I said.

"Good. Let's go into the kitchen."

I followed her.

"Here's the list and some coupons. This should be enough money." She handed me three twenty-dollar bills. "Don't you do anything except read the list. Let the robot do his work."

"Beep. I mean, okay." I laughed. Robot language was contagious.

"Robot Chad, let's go," I said, as I opened the back door.

He picked up the tray and brought it to me.

"We're going shopping for Aunt Elise now," I told him.

"And when you come back," said Aunt Elise, coming to the door to take the tray, "I'll fix some lunch for all of us. Will that be all right with the two of you?"

"Yes," I said.

"Beep," said Chad.

"I hope you don't mind driving," I said. "Aunt Elise doesn't drive, and my dad took our car."

"Beep," replied Chad.

"You do mind?"

Chad frowned. "Does not compute?" he said.

"It's not easy to talk with a robot." I laughed.

"Beep." Chad opened the car door for me.

At the market, I tried not to talk too much while Chad pushed the cart through the aisles. I thought he'd be embarrassed to have to say "beep" or "does not compute" in response to whatever I said. Then everyone would turn to look at us. I'd be embarrassed, too, I thought.

When we stepped into the checkout line, I looked at the list. "I keep thinking I've forgotten something." I marked off items in our basket. "It seems as if we have everything on the list."

"Beep, beep, beep," said Chad.

Several people turned to look at him, but he simply smiled at them.

"I did forget something?" I asked.

"Beep," said Chad.

"What?"

Chad left me in line. He went toward the produce section. I scanned the list again: lettuce, tomatoes, one cucumber, three potatoes, apples, oranges. All those things were in the basket. I moved forward in the checkout line. Where was Chad? I stood on tiptoe trying to see over the crowds waiting in the checkout lines. Then I saw him hurrying back toward me. There were so many people, I could only catch a glimpse of the top of his head as he weaved his way around shoppers and carts.

"Beep." When he reached me he held out a single daisy wrapped in green tissue. He'd been at the cut-flower display.

"For me?" I know it was a dumb thing to say, but it was the only thing I could think of.

Chad smiled. "Beep," he said.

"Thank you." I looked into his sparkling brown eyes. "Will you tell me what I did to deserve this?"

"Beep," said Chad.

"Mommy, did you hear what that man said?" A little girl sitting in the front of a shopping cart waiting to check out at the next counter pulled on her mother's hand. "He said beep, Mommy."

I turned to look at her.

Her mother smiled and patted her on the head.

"Why did he say beep?" asked the little girl.

"Should I tell her?" I whispered to Chad.

"Beep," said Chad.

"He said it again, Mommy."

I stooped down so I was eye to eye with the little girl. "He's a robot," I said. "That's the way he talks."

"Really?" The little girl's eyes opened very wide. "Mommy," she said, loud enough for the whole store to hear, "that lady has a robot. That man is a robot. Mommy, I want a robot.''

"Not now, honey," said her mother.

I looked at Chad, unsure whether to laugh, feel embarrassed, or tell the woman to listen to her little girl.

"Does not compute," said Chad. He pushed the market basket up to the counter. It was our turn to check through.

At home, while Chad carried the groceries in, I put my flower in a bud vase and placed it in the center of the table. Aunt Elise served sandwiches, coffee, and banana-walnut cake.

"This was a good lunch," I said, when we'd finished eating.

"Beep, beep, beep," agreed Chad.

"You're welcome, welcome, welcome," Aunt Elise said. "Now there's one more job to finish. The weeding."

"Come on, robot." I pushed my chair back. "I'll show you which are weeds and which are flowers."

"You mean he doesn't know?" asked Aunt Elise, a horrified expression on her face.

"No. At least that's what I think he said," I told her.

"Then you be sure to supervise him closely. I don't want my new seedlings pulled up."

"I'll stay right with him, Aunt Elise." I didn't mind at all.

The afternoon passed quickly. Benedict alternated between sleeping and begging for affection. I pointed out the weeds, and Chad pulled them. We finished the whole garden by five-thirty.

"One-half hour left before you cease to become

a robot," I said, somewhat reluctantly. "Let's wash our hands, then I'll ask Aunt Elise if she has any more assignments."

"Beep." Chad brushed the dirt from his hands, then followed me into the house.

"I do have one more thing that I'd like done. I need someone to eat another slice of banana cake and drink some milk," said Aunt Elise. "Can this robot do that?"

"Beep, beep," replied Chad.

"I thought so." Aunt Elise fed us once more. "You be sure to come again. I like a young person who eats the way you do, Chad."

"Beep," said Chad.

I glanced from Aunt Elise to Chad. Did that mean that he liked to eat or that he'd come again? Though having a robot was fun, I'd be glad when his vocabulary expanded. The novelty of beeps and does not computes was quickly wearing off.

"Time's up," said Aunt Elise, when she poured a second glass of milk for each of us. "You've done a lot of work here today, young man. Would you like to stay for dinner?"

"Does not—I mean, thank you, but my mother's expecting me home," Chad replied. "Boy, it's hard not being able to talk. Thanks for everything, Carolyn, Mrs. . . . ." He hesitated.

"Call me Aunt Elise. Everyone does," said my aunt.

That was news to me. Aunt Elise had changed lately . . . or had I changed? Maybe we both had.

"Aunt Elise, you are some good cook," Chad said.

"You're programmed—is that the right word

for a robot?—to say all the right things," said Aunt Elise.

Chad laughed as he stood up. "I have to leave," he said.

"Carolyn, you walk your ex-robot to the door. I have to see how the roast is doing in the oven," said Aunt Elise.

"Thanks for the daisy," I said as we walked toward the door. "It was a surprise."

"It was for being so nice to me. You could have made it pretty miserable and embarrassing for me today—especially at the market."

"But I wouldn't do anything like that."

We'd reached the front door. I wished I didn't have to open it and that he didn't have to leave. But there wasn't any way I knew to make him stay.

"I know you wouldn't," Chad said. "I've enjoyed being your robot. How about letting me be your friend? What are you doing tonight?"

"Studying." Why had I said that? It just seemed to jump out of my mouth.

"Does not compute," Chad responded. "Let me pick you up for a movie about eight. All right?"

"But—" What was the matter with me? When he was a robot, I talked without any problem. Now I was saying all the wrong things.

"You can study tomorrow. Eight?"

"Beep," I said shyly.

Chad laughed. "All right. I'll see you later." He opened the front door and ran down the walk. When he reached the car, he waved to me.

I smiled and waved back, then watched until the

car was gone. In slow motion, I closed the door and wandered toward the kitchen.

"Aunt Elise, Chad asked me to go to a movie tonight," I said.

"I'm not surprised." She turned the oven off. "Will you set the table, dear? We'll eat as soon as your father gets home. You won't have a lot of time to get ready."

"Do you think Daddy will mind that I didn't ask him?"

"I think he'll be glad to hear what a nice boy Chad Bennington is," replied Aunt Elise, "and I'll be sure to tell him. Don't you worry, Carolyn."

I hugged Aunt Elise. "Thanks," I said. "Aunt Elise, you're super."

"The silverware and dishes are waiting. I hear a car in the drive now."

I hurried to set the table. Chad had asked me out. Chad had asked me out, I said to myself with each place setting. And I knew just what I was going to wear.

❧ Seven ❧

I was finally ready. Feeling eager but nervous, I glanced out my bedroom window. Chad should be here in a few minutes, I thought. Going to the mirror, I checked my hair one more time. Pink was my best color, and tonight my skin had a pink glow, both from the day spent outside and from the excitement and anticipation of a date with Chad.

Suddenly the doorbell rang, putting an end to my daydreaming.

I picked up my purse from the edge of the dresser, grabbed my white sweater from the doorknob, took a deep breath, and walked as slowly as I could manage—which didn't seem slow at all —from my room to the front hall.

Aunt Elise had just opened the door. "Good evening," she said. "Here comes Carolyn."

"Hello," said Chad. He was wearing blue cotton pants and a white shirt, which showed off his tan. He'd traded his old tennis shoes for deck shoes.

"Hi," I said. "Will you come into the living room and meet my father?"

"Sure." His smile helped me relax. He didn't seem nervous at all, but I certainly was.

Aunt Elise preceded us. "Tom, the young man who did all that work for us is here to take Carolyn to the movies."

My father put the newspaper down and stood up.

"Daddy, this is Chad Bennington. Chad, this is my father, Dr. Tom Dawson."

Chad and my father shook hands.

"A pleasure," said my father. "I hear that you did quite a job today. Even the garden weeds got pulled. They'd have roped me into doing that, except I don't know a weed from a flower."

Chad looked at me and I laughed. "Neither does Chad," I said. "I had to show him which was which."

"Well, I can't seem to learn," said my father, and I thought he winked.

"We should leave so we won't miss the start of the show. We'll stop for pizza after, but we won't be too late, sir," Chad said.

"Just be sensible," replied my father. "Have a nice evening."

"Thanks, Daddy." I kissed him.

Aunt Elise walked to the front door with us. "You two have a good time. You deserve it after all the work you did today."

"Thank you. We will," said Chad.

In the car, I sat with my hands clasped in my

lap. Carolyn, I lectured myself, relax. Just because he can say more than "beep" or "does not compute" is no reason to get nervous. I glanced at Chad as he started the car.

He caught me looking and smiled. "I thought we'd see the newest movie in the *Star Wars* series, unless you've already seen it."

"I haven't."

Think of something else to say. Ask a question, I told myself, as we drove. I searched for something to say. What did everyone talk about at school? College and graduation.

"What are you doing after graduation?" I asked.

"I've been accepted at the university. I'm going to major in business or law, I'm not sure which one yet. How about you?"

"I'm going to the university, too. I want to study art."

"Nice. We'll be going there together. And you'll do well in art. I really liked those posters you did for the raffle."

"Thanks." We'd be going to college together. I smiled and sighed. I don't know if that made Chad happy, but it made me happy. Maybe— Whoa, Carolyn. One step at a time. Spend one day with a boy and you're counting your chickens, as Aunt Elise would say.

Chad eased the car into a parking spot across the street from the theater. "Let's get in line," he said. "Everyone had the same idea tonight."

The line looked as if it extended for miles. We walked at least two blocks and still hadn't reached the end.

"Carolyn! Chad!"

I looked around.

"It's Fred and Brita," Chad said. "Come on."

They were in line near the end.

"Hi," said Brita.

"Beep, beep, beep," Fred said.

"Beep, beep," answered Chad.

"No secret conferences, you two," Brita teased.

Fred winked at her. "Does not compute," he said. "Did Carolyn make you work hard?"

"Terrible," replied Chad.

"I—" Then I saw that he was grinning. "Show them the blisters."

"Uh-oh. Will grass stains do?" he asked.

"Did you have to pull weeds?" asked Fred.

"Right. You, too?"

"And clean out the attic, paint the fence, trim the hedge, and wash windows."

"Mrs. Olston got her money's worth," said Brita.

"So did I," I said.

"I started out by giving Benedict a bath," Chad said.

"Oh, no!" Brita laughed. "I wish I'd been there to watch." She turned to Fred. "Benedict is Carolyn's pony-sized dog."

"And I take it that Benedict doesn't like baths," Fred said.

"You take it right," replied Chad.

We moved forward with the line, while Chad gave a rundown of the rest of his day.

"I think you had it easier, despite Benedict," said Fred.

"How did you get along with Aunt Elise?" asked Brita.

"She's great, and can she bake." Chad took my hand. "I might even be tempted to come over and give Benedict another bath, if Carolyn will invite me."

"Anytime," I heard myself answer.

Chad squeezed my hand, and he didn't let go.

"Is that the same Aunt Elise I know, Carolyn?" Brita looked at me as if she couldn't believe what she was hearing.

"Aunt Elise is on a special campaign. She's decided she was too much of a fuddy-duddy and is undergoing an amazing reformation. Besides, Brita, you hardly slow down long enough to talk to Aunt Elise when you come over."

"I guess I do sort of dash in and out. When and how did this reform happen?" asked Brita.

"It's a long story. I'll tell you some other time."

"I can't wait. But then, maybe Chad simply charmed her. He can do that, you know." Her eyes twinkled knowingly.

She'd noticed we were holding hands, I knew. I glanced away, pretending to see how far the line had to move yet before we reached the ticket window. My face was burning . . . and not from my sunburn, either.

Finally the line did move. We bought refreshments, then found seats together on the left side of the theater. The movie started with a burst of music and a view of the galactic sky. Every once in a while, my fingers touched Chad's as we both reached for popcorn at the same time. I was caught up in the movie, and yet never lost awareness of Chad's shoulder pressing mine.

"Eating time," announced Fred, when the lights went on.

"Oh, the movie was so good," said Brita. "Didn't you just love it?"

"Yes, I just loved it," Fred teased, pulling her into a hug and imitating her. "Let's get out of here before everyone gets the same idea, and we have to wait in line to eat, too."

"Did you like the movie, Carolyn?" Chad asked as we followed Fred and Brita up the aisle.

"I thought it was terrific," I said.

He grabbed my hand and squeezed gently.

I squeezed back.

Fred was right about there being a crowd at the pizza place. We sat at a round table covered with a red-and-white-checked tablecloth. A red candle lamp flickered in the center of the table. The air was saturated with the scents of pepperoni, cheese, oregano, and tomato blended into a mouth-watering aroma. The line had already formed to wait.

"So when do we start on the mural, Chad?" Brita asked when we'd placed our order.

"As soon as I get the supplies. Carolyn, would you go with me to buy them? I don't know much about colors and types of paint or even what brushes we'll need over and above what we have at school."

"I'd be glad to help," I replied.

"Oh, you were going to help anyway," Fred informed me. "We need someone who knows how to draw and paint working on this project."

"The whole senior art class is going to help," said Chad.

"I painted my bedroom last year," Brita said.

"Wonderful. We'll put you on roller detail," Chad told her.

"What did you think of Derrick's winning drawing, Carolyn?" Brita asked, after making a face at Chad.

"I haven't seen it yet," I replied.

"It's that robot in a cap and gown tucked in the corner of the picture that makes it work for me," said Fred.

"He put a robot in his picture?" I asked. Why hadn't I thought of that? It was that special touch that said our class was here.

"Mm-hmm," said Chad. "There is the United States and the state of South Carolina flag in the background. Magnolia and dogwood blossoms are sketched around the edge, mostly at the bottom, I think. Lines of graduates are marching from between the overlap of the flags. Some carry diplomas and others carry the torch of learning, the book of knowledge, the scroll of wisdom, the staff of understanding, and our school banner."

"I'm eager to take a look at it," I said. "I wonder if Mr. Van Lawrence will try to talk Derrick into taking art. He doesn't, you know."

"No kidding!" said Fred.

"I can't wait to see the mural finished," Brita said.

Just then the thick-crust pizza came. Anyone watching would have thought that we'd been starved for weeks. It was delicious.

I sipped my glass of root beer and listened while Fred told us about his arrival at the Olstons' house—with exaggeration, of course.

Chad winked at me.

I smiled back. Happiness is sharing a pizza and a good time with special people, I thought. And Chad was the most special of all.

"It's getting late." Fred looked at his watch. "We have to leave." He swiped the last bit of pepperoni from the pizza pan and popped it into his mouth.

"We do, too," said Chad.

We said good-bye to Brita and Fred, then headed for Chad's car.

"I had a good time tonight, Chad," I said, as he slid into the front seat beside me.

"Me, too. Robot day was extremely successful —better than I hoped." He winked at me. "Much better. I'm sorry we didn't go out before tonight, Carolyn. I don't know why we never got acquainted, especially since you and Brita are such good friends."

"I guess because she's involved in a lot of projects that I'm not," I said, regretting that I hadn't known Chad better before, too.

"Then we'll have to make up for lost time. I'll call you tomorrow. And Monday after school, we'll go shopping for paint. If you want to."

"I'd love to." Did he mean what I thought he meant? He wanted to go out with me again?

Chad started the car. He drove slowly, humming along with the music on the car radio.

I rested my head on the seat and closed my eyes.

I could imagine how every fairy-tale princess felt when she'd met her Prince Charming, because I felt as if I'd met mine.

Too soon we stopped in front of my house. The porch light was on and so was the living room light.

Chad turned off the motor, then let his arm rest on the back of the seat. My heart beat faster than usual as I turned to look at him. His arm slipped to my shoulders, and he leaned toward me. His lips brushed mine lightly once. Then his other arm went around me and he kissed me again. "Good night, Carolyn," he whispered, as he pulled back.

"Good night," I answered just as quietly, still aware of the feel of his lips on mine.

He walked me to the porch. "I'll call around noon tomorrow," he said.

I nodded, then went inside.

Chad kissed me. He likes me, I thought, as I watched the car pull away. I closed the door and stood there, remembering. Finally, I turned off the lights, then walked slowly to my bedroom.

As I passed Aunt Elise's room, she called, "Is that you, Carolyn?" She sounded drowsy.

"Yes," I answered quietly.

"Did you have a good time?"

"Wonderful." I sighed.

"Good night," she said.

"Good night," I answered.

And it was such a good night, I thought, as I fell on my bed, in no hurry to give up my thoughts to sleep. I took my diary from the drawer in my bedside stand. This entry had to be worded carefully, not scrawled any old way in any old words. I wanted to record each moment of my first date with Chad to have at my fingertips for savoring again and again. I didn't ever want to forget what it felt like the first time he kissed me and the first moment I knew I was falling in love.

⇜§ *Eight* §⇝

I was dreaming about Chad. He was kissing me, but his kisses were so sloppy my face was getting wet. Half-asleep I put my hand out. His nose was cold and hairy. I opened my eyes. "Benedict!"

Benedict barked and gave me another sloppy kiss. What would Chad say if he knew that in my dream he'd kissed like Benedict? He'd probably laugh, I thought.

Benedict barked again.

"All right. I'm up. I'll feed you. What time is it?" I glanced at my small alarm clock. Seven-thirty! The alarm hadn't gone off. I'd be late for school if I didn't get going. "Good dog, Benedict." I jumped out of bed and struggled into my robe.

"Good morning, Carolyn." Aunt Elise was rinsing breakfast plates. "I was about to call you."

"Benedict did the honors. I overslept." I grabbed the dog food from the cupboard.

Benedict sat down and put one paw up. He cocked his head to one side and whined.

Aunt Elise laughed. "You should put that dog on television, Carolyn. He has the best act I've ever seen."

I laughed. "He's just a starving puppy. You can see that. Come on, hungry doggy."

Benedict's tail went wump, wump against the cupboard doors, the walls, and the back door as he followed me outside. I put his bowl down, then he gobbled his food, chasing after each little piece that fell out of his dish. He didn't miss a crumb. It took a lot of food to keep such a big dog full.

Back inside, I poured myself a glass of orange juice and filled a bowl halfway with cereal. I reached for a bran muffin, still warm from the oven.

"I'll be late coming home from school today," I said. "Chad and I are going to the paint store to buy the mural supplies."

"Will you be doing the painting?"

"Some of it. The whole senior art class will be working on it. I think Mr. Van Lawrence will enlarge and transfer the sketch onto the wall for us."

"Will the work be done during school?"

"During art class and after school."

"I won't be seeing much of you then." Aunt Elise's voice sounded kind of sad, but when I looked at her she looked the same as always.

I gulped the last of my juice and jumped up from the table. "I have to run. I'm not even dressed," I said, and hurried off to get ready for school—and Chad.

•　　•　　•

The classes had seemed interminably long today. I leaned against my locker as the last few stragglers left and silence descended in the halls. Had Chad forgotten about shopping? I wondered. Mr. Van Lawrence had drawn up a list of supplies, even specifying colors. I was relieved that the responsibility for those decisions had been taken from me. No one would question the choice of the art teacher; everyone might question my choice. I'd never be comfortable being in a spotlight, I knew.

"You're looking lonesome." Chad came up behind me and slipped his arm around my waist. "Sorry I'm late. I had to deliver a report on the raffle to Mr. Olston's office and pick up the money for the paint. And then he wanted to talk to me about the graduation ceremony. I'm going to give a speech."

"Wonderful! About what?"

"I don't have the slightest idea. Let me know if you come up with one."

" 'Our Future in the Computer Age.' 'Our Future in the Age of the Robot.' Or how about 'Now That We've Left Our Mark.'?"

"Not bad. You've been hiding some of your talents, my dear. Maybe I'll suggest you give the speech."

"Not me, Chad. I get terminal stage fright."

"Do you really?"

I nodded.

"But there's nothing to be frightened of. No one is going to bite you."

"That's easy for you to say. You like talking to people. I suffer when I have to speak to a group.

Words stick in my throat. My talent is art and drawing. Yours is talking to people and making them feel at ease."

"Is that a talent? I never thought of it like that," he said. "It's just something I can do."

"From one who doesn't have it, take my word. It's a talent."

"You do wonderful things for my ego. You draw up all our plans, and I'll do all the talking."

"All right. Here's our plan for today." I held out the list. "Let's go shopping."

"An excellent idea," agreed Chad.

We walked down the hall together, our strides matching well. I wished that there were at least a few people around to see us together. That doesn't sound like someone who doesn't like the spotlight, I thought.

"You're smiling," Chad said, as he held the door open for me.

"I'm happy."

"So am I." Chad hugged me. "We make a great team."

We took a shopping cart at the entrance of the Rainbow Paint and Supply Store. Chad pushed the cart while I took the paints from the shelf.

"Did Mr. Van Lawrence put drop cloths on the list?" he asked.

"Drop cloths and paint hats."

"What do you think of these brushes?"

I was looking for the thinner on the list and turned around to look. Chad had crossed two brushes and was holding them under his nose to

make a bristly mustache. He wiggled his eyebrows.

I laughed and picked up a wide, flat wall brush.
I held it to my chin. "How about this one, sir?" I
asked in a deep voice.

He put two smaller wall brushes at the sides
of his head. "Meow. I think we should paint the
walls the color of tender mouse. What do you
think, dear?"

Using two tiny brushes for mouse ears, I said in
a squeaky voice, "Ripe cheese-yellow would be
my choice."

"Ahem. May I help you?"

I dropped the brushes and turned to look into
the stern face of a salesman with a bristly mustache not too unlike Chad's paint brush imitation.
I tried not to laugh or even smile.

"We have to choose brushes, then we'll be
ready to add up our purchases," Chad told him.
"Thank you."

"My name is Mr. Bryar. Call me if you need
help," he said in a very disapproving tone of
voice, then slowly walked away.

"You did the talking very well," I said.

"Of course. That's my talent," replied Chad.

After we picked out all the brushes, we went to
the checkout counter. As Mr. Bryar rang up our
purchases, he didn't even seem pleased at the
amount we'd spent. He still looked stern and disapproving.

"Do you think he's been old and sour forever?"
Chad said as he pushed the cart toward the car.

"Aunt Elise would say he has a bad case of

fuddy-duddiness.'' I glanced back at the store.

"I like your Aunt Elise," said Chad as we loaded the paint into the trunk of his car. "I can't imagine her being a fuddy-duddy."

"But she was," I said. "Not too long ago. And in a way it's your fault she isn't anymore."

"My fault?" Chad stared at me. "But I just met her."

I explained about the mural contest.

"It sounds to me as if it's just as much your fault," he said. "You're the one who asked her opinion."

"I guess we didn't talk very much," I said, and briefly told him about Aunt Elise coming to live with us. "Anyway, after all these years, we're finally getting to know each other."

"That's nice," said Chad. "And after all these years, we're getting to know each other, too, which is even nicer." He squeezed my hand.

I agreed, but could only smile. Suddenly I was tongue-tied again.

"Will you come in for a few minutes?" I asked when we reached my house.

"All right. I'd better call home so my parents don't get worried."

"Use the phone in the study," I said.

I closed the front door and turned around to see Benedict come racing from the direction of my room. He slid to a stop in front of me, allowing me to pet him; then he jumped on Chad, begging for attention.

"Down, Benedict," I said.

"That's okay." Chad stooped down and

scratched Benedict behind the ears and under the chin. "Did you recover from your bath, fella?" he asked.

Benedict tried to cuddle up to Chad and almost knocked him over.

"I think he likes you," I said.

"You don't know how relieved I am about that. If he didn't, we'd have a very difficult time meeting."

I'd never thought of that. Benedict was such a nice dog. I couldn't recall him not liking anyone. But if he ever were to dislike someone . . . *difficult* wouldn't be an adequate word to describe the problems it could cause.

"Can we take him for a walk?" asked Chad.

"He'd love it. Make your call. I'll tell Aunt Elise where we're going and get the leash." I pointed the way to the study.

"Would you like some stale bread to feed the ducks at the park?" Aunt Elise asked, when she heard that we were going to walk Benedict.

"Sure. I just hope we can keep Benedict from eating it."

"Try to keep him from eating the ducks, too. Keep him on the leash," advised Aunt Elise.

"Don't worry. We will."

"Hello, Aunt Elise. How's my favorite cookie baker?" Chad poked his head around the corner of the kitchen door.

"That's a hint if I ever heard one. The cookie jar is on the counter, young man. Don't take them all or Tom will be upset. He likes cookies and milk before bed."

"I don't want to upset Carolyn's dad. I'll just

have one cookie," said Chad.

"Take two," Aunt Elise said.

Benedict followed Chad around the kitchen and whined.

"Oh, all right," said Aunt Elise. She gave Benedict a cookie, too.

"Just remember that Benedict had a cookie, too, when Mr. Dawson asks where they went," Chad said.

"What? You're going to blame Benedict?" I asked.

"Would you rather I blamed you?" asked Chad, holding out a cookie for me to take a bite.

"You two—you three—get out of here. I'll bake some more cookies if you'll get out from under my feet," said Aunt Elise.

"In that case, I'll take another one," Chad said.

Aunt Elise pretended to smack his hand as he put the lid back on the cookie jar. "Do you want to stay for dinner, too?" she asked.

"I'd love to, but I can't. We're having company for dinner. Maybe another time?"

"Anytime you want," she said.

"Let's go before it gets too late." I snapped the leash to Benedict's collar.

His tail drooped, and he looked at me with big sad eyes; but when we headed for the front door instead of the back I guess he decided that he wasn't going to have another bath and he could be happy again. His tail went from between his legs to its normal pendulum swing.

"If you carry the bread, I'll take the leash," said Chad.

I was proud of Benedict; he behaved so well. My father had insisted that Benedict go to obedience school when he saw how big the dog was growing. If Benedict didn't know how to behave, no one could have walked him.

The park was four blocks down and two blocks over from my house. The late-afternoon sun made the sky glow with a soft pink radiance. The scent of early-blooming jasmine floated on the air. I loved spring.

We turned down the park path. Other people were out enjoying the beauty of the afternoon. Children chased each other across the lawns, emerald with new growth. A group of boys were trying to fly a kite, but there wasn't enough wind to scoop it up into the air.

Benedict sniffed along the path, his tail in continuous motion.

Chad took my hand as we rounded the turn that led toward the pond.

When we reached the irregular-shaped body of water with its few cattails growing at the edge, Chad pointed to a bench near the water's edge. "We'll tie Benedict there, then we can feed the ducks," he said.

There were no other people around in this section of the park. I slipped my shoes off and pushed them under the bench. The grass felt cool and soft under my toes.

At first Benedict barked at the ducks and strained to get at them.

"Sit, Benedict. Stay," I commanded.

He obeyed, but his body leaned forward and his tail never stopped. He wanted to play with the ducks. I knew, however, that the ducks didn't want to play with him. A few of the larger ones hissed and flapped their wings at him.

I opened the bag of bread and handed some pieces to Chad. We broke them into small chunks and tossed them at the edge of the water.

"Look, Chad." I pointed toward the cattails. A mother and three ducklings swam into view. We both tossed bread crumbs to them.

Other ducks crowded along the bank, trying to snatch some of the treats. The mother duck stayed where she was, and Chad continued to throw bread to her, while I kept the other ducks busy. It was fun to watch the babies tip themselves over so only their tails were visible.

When the bread was gone, a couple of ducks squabbled over the last few pieces, then they all swam away.

Benedict was stretched out beside the bench with his head on his paws.

"He looks insulted," said Chad, as we went back to the bench.

"He shouldn't be. He had a cookie before we came." My feet were getting cold so I slipped my shoes on again.

At the word *cookie* Benedict looked up.

"He sure understands you." Chad put his arm around me, and I let my head rest on his shoulder. As the sun moved down, shadows fell across the pond.

"I could sit here for hours," I murmured.

"I know what you mean. There's something so peaceful and relaxing about green and trees and water."

And there's something so nice about having your arm around me, I thought.

I wondered if Chad was thinking something similar. He hugged me right then.

We sat there for a while, just watching the ducks and the other people who came to feed them. We didn't talk much, but our silence wasn't awkward the way silence sometimes is when two people are together.

"I guess we'd better go back," said Chad, as the sun began to go down.

"I guess," I agreed with a sigh.

We untied Benedict. Chad slipped his arm around me, then we walked slowly back along the paths we'd come. Before we reached the edge of the park, he kissed me—just a small kiss on the forehead—but it was a kiss that said a lot. It said that I was special.

⇜ *Nine* ⇝

On Tuesday the art class gathered around Mr. Van Lawrence and watched while he sketched the mural on the wall. He explained how he had increased the scale of each figure to transfer it from the original drawing.

Then our work started. At first it was difficult to tell just what each part was going to be as various sections were painted. But it was exciting to pass this wall at the end of each day and see what progress had been made.

Art students weren't the only ones working on the mural. Derrick was there, of course, and so were the student council members. Mr. Van Lawrence had jobs for everyone, paints to be mixed and carried, brushes to be cleaned, drop clothes to be spread.

I was part of a school project for the first time. How much fun had I missed during my high school days? I wondered, as I listened to some of the comments and jokes that went on during our work. If I'd signed up for other projects, become more involved, would I have had more fun? Now I wouldn't know, but I'd always have the mural to remember.

On Friday, I rode home with Brita, Fred, and Chad. "I can't wait to see that mural finished," Brita said. "It's better than I ever imagined."

"Seeing it painted is sort of like unwrapping a package a section at a time," said Chad. "The suspense builds and your imagination pictures what's ahead." He handed me my books as Fred pulled up in front of my house. "I'll call you tonight, Carolyn. Don't plan anything for tomorrow until you talk to me."

"That sounds like an order," I said.

"A strong suggestion?"

"All right." I waved as they drove off, then ran up the walk.

The mail was spread across the floor. I bent and picked it all up. There were ads and some bills. But there were also two catalogs, both from art schools. I hadn't sent for these. I turned them over. They were addressed to Aunt Elise.

"Anyone home?" I called.

There was no answer, but I heard Benedict bark and scratch at the back door. I went in that direction.

Aunt Elise was out back cutting flowers. "I'm home," I called.

"Is it that late already?" She stood up and pushed her large straw hat back on her head. She held a bright bouquet in her hand. "I guess this will fill our vase."

She came inside, hung the hat on a hook inside

the back door, then went into the kitchen, where she took a milk-glass vase from the cupboard.

I took an apple from the bowl on the counter and sat at the table. "The mail came," I told her. "There's something interesting for you."

"For me?" She moved flowers from one side of the vase to the other, each time standing back to look at her work.

"Catalogs. From art schools."

"Oh." She glanced at me and rearranged two more flowers. "I sent for them after our little talk. You're so busy with Chad and will be going off to college next fall, and your father doesn't need much done for him, so I thought maybe . . . maybe I'd take a class or two." She sounded so uncertain.

I jumped up from the table and hugged her. "I think that's wonderful," I said.

"You don't think I'm too old?"

"You're never too old, Aunt Elise. Why don't we look at the catalogs now?"

She placed the vase in the center of the table. "Let's," she agreed.

She sat beside me, and we pored over both books.

"There's a lot to choose from," she said. "How will I know where to start? I don't even know if I want a correspondence course or if I want to go right to the school."

"You could talk to a counselor," I said.

"A counselor? What will I talk about?"

"What kind of goals you have. What your interests are. How much you know and how much you want to learn."

"But what if I don't know? This is so new."

"I know, Aunt Elise. I have the same feelings."

"But you're young and confident."

"I'm young, but I'm never confident," I told her.

"I don't know about that," said Aunt Elise. "That boy who comes around is very nice. That's enough to make any girl confident."

"Chad? I never thought about feeling confident because of him."

"Well, you should. He's chosen you."

"But we're not going together or anything. He's just asked me out a couple of times—once to buy paint for the mural, so that doesn't even count."

"And what about all the other time he spends here? And those hours on the telephone? That counts for a lot. It hasn't been that long since I was a girl."

"He likes your cookies and he likes to talk."

Aunt Elise shook her head and smiled. Brita was right. Chad had charmed Aunt Elise.

"Aunt Elise, did you ever have a boyfriend?" I asked, suddenly curious.

Aunt Elise sighed. "Once," she replied.

"Will you tell me about him?"

She folded her hands on top of the catalog and seemed to be staring far away to a place and time that I couldn't see.

"I met him at the office where I worked. His name was William. We were engaged."

"What happened?" I asked.

"We were supposed to be married in June. I'd started shopping for a gown—nothing too fancy or expensive, just a beautiful bridal gown. But I hadn't bought it yet.

"We went out to dinner and a show one evening. William had been working some long hours. He was tired, but he insisted we go out.

"After he left me at the house, he ran a stop sign going home. He was killed instantly by the truck that hit his car." Aunt Elise covered her face with her hands.

I put my arm around her shoulders. "I'm sorry," I said. "I didn't know."

"I still have his ring in my jewelry box," she said softly. "It was a long time ago, but there was never anyone else."

The phone rang. "I'll get it." I went into the study to answer, so Aunt Elise could be alone. She'd had a lot of disappointment and heartache in her life, I realized, some of it probably caused by me. For a long time I had resented her trying to take my mother's place.

"Hello," I said.

"Carolyn, are you okay? You sound kind of sad."

"I'm fine, Chad. Aunt Elise and I were just having a discussion about college and other things."

"Oh. Shall I call back?"

"No. That's all right."

"Are you busy tomorrow?"

"Not yet."

"Would you like to go into town for the day? We can wander through the open-air market, and I'll buy lunch at the Ice House."

"You mean play tourist?"

"Sure. Maybe Brita and Fred would like to come along."

"All right. Ask them. That sounds like fun."

"I'll pick you up at nine."

I hung up and went back to the kitchen. "That was Chad. He wants to go into town tomorrow. We're going to the Market and have lunch. Brita and Fred might go, too."

"Maybe you can buy some fruit for me," said Aunt Elise. She closed the catalogs. "I'll think about these before I do anything more."

"Don't think too long, Aunt Elise. You should sign up soon."

She nodded. "I have to get dinner started. Will you set the table, Carolyn?"

"Sure," I said.

It wasn't long before we heard the familiar, "The captain's home."

During dinner I told my father about the mural and our Saturday plans.

"You're seeing quite a bit of this one boy, aren't you?" he asked.

"We go to school together, Daddy," I said.

"And he comes over here and he calls and tomorrow you're spending the day with him."

"I like him. Brita and Fred are going with us tomorrow, too."

My father sighed. "Elise?" he said, in a tone of voice that sounded like he was saying, "Help!"

"The boy is all right, Tom. Carolyn has enough sense not to rush into anything. They're both planning on going to college."

"Rush into anything! Daddy! Aunt Elise!"

"Don't sound so shocked, Carolyn," my father said. "I was young once, too. I know how it is. I have a duty as your father—"

"Tom, would you like some more chicken?" my aunt interrupted.

He looked from Aunt Elise to me. "All right. No lectures. Just know that I care about you and what you do."

"I know you do, Daddy. Don't worry."

"Don't worry," he said, as he took his plate from Aunt Elise. "How can a parent not do that?"

The next morning, I slept later than I'd planned, so I had to rush to get ready. I was still getting dressed when Fred, Brita, and Chad arrived. Quickly I put on my blue skirt, white T-top, and sandals, and ran downstairs.

"Don't forget the fruit, Carolyn," said Aunt Elise as I said good-bye.

"I won't," I promised and hurried to join my friends.

"I'd like to buy your aunt a present," Chad said, once we were on our way.

"Aunt Elise?" asked Brita, sounding surprised.

"Mm-hmm. I'll know the right thing when I see it," Chad said.

"I thought he was going out with you, Carolyn. Now I'm beginning to wonder," said Brita.

"Aunt Elise likes him, too," I said.

It took a while to find a parking place in town and we ended up several blocks away from the

Market, but I didn't mind the walk. The historic
part of Charleston fascinated me. The houses were
old, some of them even open for tours to the curious public. Earthquake rods with their circular or
sometimes decorative ends poked from the sides
of the bricks, testimony to the great earthquake
that had made us almost as famous as San Fran-
cisco.

The Market was three blocks long and dated
back to the early 1800s. Under the roofs were a
few shops and lots of long wooden tables filled
with various wares ranging from antiques to
woven baskets made right before your eyes.

Brita bought a cloisonné medallion. Fred
bought an ornate belt buckle. They wandered
away to look while Chad and I walked slowly to
browse. We stopped beside a table of shell
jewelry. "That one," said Chad, pointing.

"For Aunt Elise?" I asked, looking at the
delicate pink shells strung on an almost invisible
string.

"For you," he said.

"But Chad—"

"No buts." He paid for the necklace then put it
around my neck. "Just right," he said.

I peered into the small square mirror at the
end of the table and touched the necklace. It was
pretty.

"Thank you. Now I should buy something for
you," I said.

"But—" he began.

"No buts," I told him, as firmly as he had told
me.

We walked slowly again while I looked. Then I

saw the right gift. Nothing too personal, but something with meaning. "I'll take that," I said to the man.

"Cute little thing, isn't it?" He held up my selection.

I nodded in agreement. "Chad, you'll never forget our first Saturday together," I said.

Chad laughed when he saw what I'd chosen. "Someone was watching," he said, as he looked at the ceramic statue of a sad-looking dog sitting in a tub of suds. "Poor Benedict."

With our treasures purchased, we hurried to catch up with Fred and Brita. They were talking with a lady selling baskets who was showing them how she wove the reeds back and forth to make a design.

"Are you two ready to eat?" asked Chad.

"Oh, wait. I have to buy some fruit for Aunt Elise. I want to get it before the good stuff is gone," I said.

"We'll get a table at the Ice House. Meet us there," said Fred.

I selected some nice fruit, which Chad offered to carry, and then we went to meet Brita and Fred.

"After lunch, I want to go into one of the shops," said Chad. "I think I can find a gift for Aunt Elise there."

"Which one?" I asked.

"You'll see," he said. "It will be a surprise."

The Ice House was crowded. While we waited for a waitress to take our order, I looked around. The walls were decorated with old ice tongs, picks, and lanterns. The front door was like a huge old ice box door. The front of the menu was printed like an old newspaper and told the history of the Market and how ice used to be brought from frozen northern lakes to Charleston on sailing schooners packed with sawdust. Carts pulled the ice to storage houses with thick walls, where it was sold to shoppers at the market.

"This is really interesting," I said, putting the menu down on the table. "Can't you imagine living here long ago?"

"You do get that feeling in this part of town," agreed Brita. "I'm not sure I would have liked wearing those long dresses, though, especially in the summer."

"Did you see the back of the menu?" asked Fred, after the waitress came to take our orders. "There were old advertisements. Some of them were rewards offered for runaway slaves."

"That doesn't seem real at all. I can't imagine it," said Brita.

"I couldn't have owned another person," Chad said.

We were all quiet for a few minutes. So many of these streets and buildings had witnessed history, both the good and bad of it, I thought. What would people a hundred years from now be saying and doing on this same spot? Would our times be considered better or worse? It was a spooky thought.

"In the year 2084," predicted Chad, as if reading my mind, "people will send their robots to the market."

"Aunt Elise is way ahead of time, then," I said.

Chad laughed. "I forgot about that."

After lunch, we went to the shops. Chad led the

way into a gourmet cook shop. "There's the gift for Aunt Elise," he said. "Does she have a fancy cookie press?"

"I don't think so," I replied.

"This one." Chad chose a ceramic stamp with the face of a sun carved on it. "Her cookies warm my insides," he said.

"Oh," groaned Fred.

"I think that's cute," Brita said.

"I'll make a card for you, Chad, and write that on the inside."

"That would be great, Carolyn. I'm ready to go home now. I can't wait to see Aunt Elise's face when she opens her gift."

As we drove home, we talked of our day in town. Brita was more determined than ever to get a job as a tour guide. "I'm going to come back here next weekend and apply at every place I can," she said.

"What are you doing for the summer, Carolyn?" asked Chad.

"I'll probably work in the office at the medical university. My dad got me a job there last year. How about you and Fred?"

"I'll be starting a new job at the garage—working some weekends," said Fred. "It's better than the drugstore where I work now for only a couple of afternoons a week."

"I'm going to caddy at the golf club," Chad said.

"Plush job," commented Fred. "How did you get in there?"

"The neighbor next door works in the pro shop."

"This will be our last summer before college," said Brita. "Sure seems strange that high school is almost over."

"Scary," I said.

Chad slipped his arm around me. "We'll be together at the university," he said. "I think."

"You think? I thought you were accepted already."

"Oh, I was. But my dad keeps bugging me to go and see the college he graduated from up in Massachusetts. He won't let up until I do. I promised I'd go with him when they have their spring open house in a couple weeks." He hugged me. "Don't look so worried. I won't change my mind."

"Especially now that you're going to the university, too, Carolyn," said Brita.

"True," Chad whispered in my ear. "I want us to be together." He kissed me and his lips told me that he meant what he said.

"Come over tonight for a few minutes. I'll have the card ready, and you can surprise Aunt Elise," I said.

"About eight?" asked Chad.

"Perfect."

He kissed me quickly, then I slid out of the car. "See you later."

"Later," he repeated.

I ran up the walk.

At eight o'clock the doorbell rang. I hurried to answer. "Come in the study," I said, pulling Chad down the hall.

My father was sitting in the wing chair reading

the paper. "Good evening, Chad," he said. "What are you two up to?"

"Good evening, sir."

"Here. Sign." I handed the card I'd made to Chad. On the front I'd drawn a heart-shaped cookie jar. Inside I'd written his sentiment.

"This is perfect," he said. "Thanks, Carolyn."

"Aren't you going to let me in on this?" asked my father.

"Sure, Daddy." Quickly I explained.

"I want to watch. Elise is in her room. I'll send her to the kitchen. You two go on ahead."

"Daddy likes a good surprise, too," I said, as we entered the kitchen.

"Sometimes I'm not too sure he likes me, though," said Chad. "I see him looking at me and frowning."

"He likes you. It's just . . ."

"Just what?" asked Chad, as we sat down at the table.

"He's not used to me having a—a boyfriend," I finished. I hoped I hadn't said too much calling Chad my boyfriend. Did he think of me as his girlfriend?

"Well, I hope he does get used to it." Chad put his hand over mine. "Because that's the way it is."

"What's the trouble?" Aunt Elise came into the kitchen. She was carrying one of the school catalogs. My father came right behind her.

"No trouble, Aunt Elise. I have something for you." Chad held out a package. "I wrapped it myself."

"For me? Why?"

"The card will tell you why," he said.

Aunt Elise sat down and opened the card. " 'Your cookies warm my insides,' " she read. "Well, I'm glad to hear that. You've eaten so many, you could have had indigestion. You didn't mean burn, did you?"

"Elise!" exclaimed my father, sounding surprised.

"I'm only teasing, Tom," she said.

"You haven't teased like that since we were kids," he muttered. "But you really gave it to me then."

I made a mental note to ask my dad some questions. "Open the present," I said, feeling like a little kid at a party.

"All right. I will." Aunt Elise seemed to take forever to loosen the paper and open the box. "Oh. How clever! Your cookies warm my insides. Look, Tom. A sun. Well I'll just stamp out a batch of sugar cookies tomorrow. Thank you, Chad."

"You're welcome."

I'd never seen Chad blush before.

"That was a nice thought," said my father. He was smiling and so was I.

❧ *Ten* ❧

April eased into May.

"We should complete the mural in another week," Mr. Van Lawrence announced, when we had put in a couple of hours after school on Wednesday. "Derrick, is this shaping up the way you pictured?"

"Better." Derrick seemed almost embarrassed when Mr. Van Lawrence spoke to him. He was a quiet boy, but I wasn't sure if it was because that's the way he always was or because he was working with a bunch of talkative seniors. When you put Fred, Brita, Chad, and Toni together, there was rarely a moment's silence.

I also noticed that Derrick had his own fan club. Two sophomore girls, Lonette and Charity, spent a lot of time watching Derrick's mural take shape on the wall.

Everyone on today's mural crew stood back to admire our progress. All that was left were some outlines and finishing touches. The mural looked great! It didn't even bother me anymore that I hadn't won the contest. Helping to paint made this mural almost as much mine as it was Derrick's.

"Don't anyone plan anything for a week from this Saturday," said Toni. "I'm having a mural party at my house. You're all invited. Including your faithful friends over there, Derrick, if you want to ask them."

Derrick smiled. "I might," he replied.

The two girls giggled when he turned to look at them.

"I don't know if I can make it," said Chad.

"Why? Where are you going?" I asked.

"To that open house at my dad's college. We're flying up Friday night and will come back sometime late Saturday. You go to the party anyway, Carolyn."

"Oh, yes. Be sure to come," said Toni.

"Fred and I will give you a ride," Brita offered.

"Good. That's settled," Toni said. "I hope the rest of you are planning to come."

A party without Chad. I wasn't sure I wanted to go alone.

We cleaned up the drop cloths, put the paints and brushes away, and promised Mr. Van Lawrence to work again the next afternoon.

"Let's take Benedict to the park," Chad said, as we walked across the student lot to his car.

"Great idea. Some shade and relaxation sounds good right now."

Chad patted my hand. "The mural is almost finished. It does take a lot of time, doesn't it?"

"Oh, I don't really mind." I glanced at him.

"Especially since we're working together."

Chad nodded. "I'm sorry I won't be here for Toni's party. How about if we do something special this Saturday, though—a picnic by the pond. Just the two of us."

"All right. Maybe Aunt Elise will make some cookies to warm your insides."

He turned left out of the parking lot. "Do you think so? What if we invited her?"

"Just the two of us," I reminded him.

"Right," he said. "But for cookies . . ."

"Chad Bennington, you'd trade me for cookies?" I tried to sound hurt.

"I didn't exactly say that."

"You did, too."

He stopped the car at a stop sign and leaned over to kiss me. "Never. You're sweeter than cookies."

"That sounds like a line."

"I mean it." He kissed me again, then a car behind us honked. "But if they were chunky chocolate-chip cookies with pecans . . ." he said quietly.

"Aargh," I said, and he laughed.

While we rode the next couple of blocks to my house, I thought about how different everything was since I'd met Chad. Aunt Elise and I got along really well now. I was involved at school. And I could even talk to some of the popular kids without feeling so self-conscious, not that I didn't still get tongue-tied sometimes. But I never felt like that with Chad anymore. He's made the end of my senior year very special, I thought.

When we reached my house, we said hello to

Aunt Elise and put Benedict on his leash. He knew what was coming; we'd taken him along with us more than once since our first walk to the park.

Chad didn't say much as we walked down the street. He held Benedict's leash in one hand and my hand in the other.

"School will be over before long," I said, as we entered the park.

"It will be time to get serious then," said Chad. "We'll be in college."

"I wonder if college will go by as fast as high school did?"

"Maybe faster," he said.

Our bench near the pond was empty. We tied Benedict, who stretched out in the grass to nap, and sat down to watch the ducks.

The park was quiet this afternoon. The air was warm with the feel of summer. The trees were in full leaf now. A breeze whispered through their branches and rippled the pond.

"What are you thinking about?" Chad put his arm around me. "Are you still upset about being in competition with cookies?"

"Shouldn't I be?" I teased.

"No." His tone of voice was serious. "You shouldn't be, Carolyn. You have no competition. I'm nuts about cookies, but . . . I love you."

For a minute I couldn't move. I couldn't say anything, because I was overwhelmed with the emotions that leaped within me when I heard his words. Then I looked into Chad's eyes and saw that he was absolutely serious. There was no teasing twinkle behind his intent gaze, no quirk of the lips to hint at a joke to follow. "Maybe your senior year of high school isn't the best time to fall in love," he said. "There're so many decisions to make about your life. But that's what happened. You're not like any other girl I know, like any other girl I've ever dated, Carolyn. I just hope you care a little bit about me."

I touched the side of his face, then let my fingers trail down to his jaw, then across to his mouth. He kissed my fingers. "I care more than a little, Chad," I said. "I love you, too."

He pulled me into his arms, burying his face in my hair. When he looked at me again, his eyes did twinkle, not teasingly, but happily. He held me closer, and his lips met mine, speaking the language of love where no words were necessary.

There were a lot of times in my life when I'd thought I was happy. I was happy when I got Benedict, an unbelievably small puppy when you looked at him now. I was happy when I won first prize in an art contest in junior high. I was happy when I got my acceptance to the university. I was happy when Chad first asked me out. But not one of those times could compare with the way I felt at this moment. I wanted to soar straight up into the blue, cloudless sky, the way a jet plane sometimes does, with a trail stretching out behind to announce that it's there. I wanted to spread my arms and run through the park the way the children do, then fall in the grass. I felt like laughing and crying and shouting and skipping all at the same time. I couldn't sit still.

"Let's untie Benedict and go for a run," I said. "I'm too happy to sit here and watch ducks."

"You know what? I feel the same way." Chad

pulled the leash from its knot.

Although Benedict didn't seem nearly as enthusiastic as we were, he loped along with us as we crisscrossed the park paths.

Finally, out of breath, we stopped by a water fountain to get a drink. Chad made a cup with his hands and gave Benedict some water, too. He glanced at his watch. "We do have to get back home," he said. "I've got a ton of homework tonight."

"Me, too. Last-minute panic by the teachers. Quick! Be sure those seniors learn something before we let them out of this school."

Chad laughed. "Saturday we'll have a celebration picnic," he said.

"What are we celebrating?" I asked. "The mural?"

"What mural? You can celebrate that at Toni's party. We're celebrating us," he said, then put his finger on the water fountain and squirted me.

"You'll be sorry," I said, wiping water from the front of my shirt. I started to run after him, but he and Benedict had a head start. "No more cookies!" I shouted.

At that, he stopped and came back toward me.

"Chad," I said, slipping my arm around his waist, "I'll always have my doubts about you—and cookies."

"Only about chunky chocolate chips," he said and kissed me.

I hated to say good-bye. It seemed as if by saying those three beautiful words—I love you—Chad had become even more special than before, and our time together more precious.

We stood on the porch and held hands for a few minutes, then he kissed me good-bye. He handed Benedict's leash to me. "I'll see you at school tomorrow," he said.

I nodded and bent down to scratch Benedict's ears.

"What's wrong, Carolyn?"

"I wish you didn't have to go to Massachusetts next week. I hate the thought of going to Toni's party without you."

Chad sighed. "I know. I really should tell my dad that I absolutely will not change my mind about going to the university here. But I did promise. I think he really wants to go. There must be a lot of good memories there for him and Mom."

"You're sure you won't be back in time for the party?"

"I'll try. All right?"

"All right."

"Maybe I'll call you tonight, if I get my homework finished."

"Then hurry home and do it," I said, giving him a slight push.

"Hey, I thought you loved me," he said.

"Shsh. Someone will hear you." I couldn't help but laugh.

"I don't care. I think I'll shout to the whole neighborhood, the whole city, the whole state, the whole nation, the whole world—Carolyn Dawson loves Chad Bennington and Chad Bennington loves her back!" He shouted this in a loud whisper, then caught me in a hug.

"Chad, go home and do your homework."

"Can I shout real loud then?"

I laughed. "You can call me then."

He kissed me two more times, and I was sure that at least once Aunt Elise peeked out the front window. "Talk to you later," he said, then ran down the walk.

Benedict barked and whined.

"I know how you feel, puppy," I said. "I'd like to go with him or have him stay, too." I watched his car until I couldn't see even a speck of it any longer. "Come on, Benedict, time for you to eat." We went inside.

That evening Chad called, and we talked and talked. We told each other about our childhoods. I laughed until my stomach ached at some of his stories. "After me, my mother was afraid to have any more kids," he said.

We talked about middle school and Patriot High. We talked about our hopes for the future. Though our thoughts about each other and what the future would hold for us as a couple went unspoken, I knew they were there in the backs of our minds. It was just too soon to say them out loud. But that time would come if it was meant to.

When I finally hung up, I stared up at my canopy and thought about all the times I'd stretched out on my bed like this and dreamed about Prince Charming and about Chad Bennington. Sometimes dreams do come true, I thought.

The phone rang again. "Hello," I said when I picked up the receiver.

"Carolyn, is that you?"

"Mm-hmm. Hi, Brita."

"You sound half-asleep."

"No. I'm wide awake. I was just thinking."

"About Chad."

"How did you know?"

"The dreamy sound of your voice. What are you doing next Friday before Toni's party?"

"Nothing. Why?"

"Why don't you come spend the night? Fred has to work late at the garage. We can catch up on girl talk."

"All right." I had a lot to tell her.

"Super! Next question. Have you written that composition for English class?"

"I haven't opened a book yet. Just a minute." I reached for my schoolbooks, which had been spread out on my bed. My powers of concentration had all been focused on the phone since dinnertime, however. Despite my lectures to Chad to get his homework done, mine was still waiting. Brita and I spent the next half hour discussing our assignments.

"Thanks," Brita said, when we were all through. "I knew I could count on you. I'll see you at school tomorrow and don't forget next Friday."

"I won't." I hung up the phone again and rolled over. My head hung off the edge of the bed. Below me, my dog was in his usual place on the rug. "Benedict," I said, "isn't life just wonderful?"

Benedict woofed and stretched to give me a kiss.

"I still love you, too," I said, hugging his big shaggy head. "Don't worry. I love you and Chad both." Then I giggled. "But you wouldn't make a good substitute at Toni's party. You can't dance." I sat up. Chad just had to be back in time for the party. He just had to.

❦ *Eleven* ❧

"Are you sure you have enough?" Aunt Elise asked as I put the cookies and fruit in the picnic cooler.

"I have enough to feed ten people," I said, "and you know that Chad can survive on cookies alone."

Aunt Elise smiled. "Did I tell you that the new Women's Community Center is offering art classes this summer? I think I might just start my studies there."

"That's a great idea," I said. "And maybe the teacher will know something about the programs at the various schools."

Aunt Elise nodded. "I had the same thought, dear."

Benedict, who was out in the back, barked.

"Chad must be here." I ran to the front door.

"Nice outfit," he said, as he jumped from the walk to the porch.

"Thank you, kind sir." If only he knew how

many different clothes I'd tried on before deciding on my blue jumpsuit. I'd also gathered one section of my hair on the side and tied it with a blue bow, something different for a special day.

"I'm ready if you are," I said. "Come get the cooler and say hello to Aunt Elise."

He followed me into the kitchen. Outside, Benedict was barking loudly.

"Good morning, Chad. Benedict wants to go with you," said Aunt Elise.

"Good morning." Chad covered his ears at the racket coming from the backyard.

"Benedict, stop that!" I called out the window.

His barks turned to low, pitiful howls.

"We've spoiled him," I said.

"I don't mind if he comes with us," said Chad, "if you don't."

"Please," Aunt Elise said. "If I have to listen to that all day . . ."

"All right, dog. Just this once you'll get away with this." I took the leash from its hook and opened the back door.

Benedict bounded inside, his tail thrashing everything nearby. He raced over to Chad and licked his hand.

"I guess we have everything now." I clipped the leash on Benedict.

"Take some dog biscuits," suggested Aunt Elise. "Otherwise Chad will have to share his cookies."

"There's a limit," said Chad. "It's bad enough I have to share my girl."

"So that's how it is," Aunt Elise said. "Benedict, you chaperone these two."

"Aunt Elise, did you put him up to all that noise?" asked Chad.

"I may be getting old," she replied, "but I still have memories." For just a moment her eyes held a serious, faraway look. "A lot of memories," she said. "Well, out of here, you three." She walked with us as far as the front porch. "I hope your picnic doesn't get rained on. There are a lot of clouds piling up out there."

I looked, too. A sky that had been clear and blue was now edged with thick, gray clouds, the kind that could mean a thunderstorm.

"Maybe we should drive down to the park," Chad said, "just in case."

"That cooler is too heavy to carry all those blocks anyway," said Aunt Elise.

Chad opened the back door of the car, and Benedict jumped in. I slid onto the front seat. After putting the cooler and our blanket in the trunk he ran around to the driver's side. "We're off," he said. "Rain, rain, go away."

"Come again another day," I finished.

"Do you know this one?" he asked. " 'Peter, Peter, pumpkin eater' . . ."

We recited the next few lines together.

" 'And there he kept her very well,' " I finished. "A pumpkin doesn't sound like a great place to live to me."

"Think how popular your house would be on Halloween."

"Everyone would want to cut holes in the walls. I'm not convinced. My favorite nursery rhyme was always 'Mary had a little lamb' . . .''

"And the doctor fainted," Chad said with a grin.

"Ha ha. That's not how it goes."

We recited the rhyme together, then tried to remember others. There are some things that stay in your mind forever, I thought. And I knew that no matter what happened in the future, I'd never forget Chad and our love.

At the park Benedict seemed to know exactly where to go. He led the way down the paths toward the pond. We spread our blanket under a tree. The sun was still shining, and I forgot about the clouds on the horizon.

Again, we talked. Chad told me about his parents. His father owned a tool manufacturing company, his mother worked in a plant nursery. I told him more about my mother's death and the problems I'd had accepting Aunt Elise. I found out that he'd been a Boy Scout at the same time I was a Girl Scout. We'd both gone to camp and taken swimming lessons. And though we'd gone to separate elementary and middle schools, finally meeting at high school, we'd often been at the same place at the same time without knowing it.

"Just think, we were probably both in line to see Santa Claus at the same time," he said.

I nodded. "And we both swam in the Y swim festival."

"Maybe you were that little girl who beat me in the free-style," he said.

"Not me. I didn't want to swim. Aunt Elise made me. So I didn't try. I came in second to last."

We ate fat chicken-salad sandwiches with crisp lettuce, which Benedict insisted on sharing. I poured iced tea from the Thermos and there were potato chips, cookies, apples, and the first of the season's strawberries, which Chad and I took turns feeding to each other.

"Good strawberries," he said, kissing me between bites.

"You taste like a strawberry," I said.

"Because I'm sweet."

Benedict whined and edged closer to us on the blanket. A minute later thunder rumbled off in the distance. A couple of warning drops bounced off the cooler.

"Uh-oh," said Chad. "He heard that thunder before we did."

"We'd better pack up," I said. "Sitting under a tree in a thunderstorm is dangerous."

I repacked the picnic cooler, while Chad folded the blanket and soothed Benedict, who was quivering at the repeated rolls of thunder moving closer. The air had grown still and felt heavy.

"Let's hurry," he said. "When the rain comes, it's going to be a good storm."

Benedict led the way as we ran to the car.

We weren't inside more than a minute when the first fat drops splashed on the windshield.

"So much for our picnic," I said. "At least we were almost finished eating."

"This isn't so bad. It's cozy." Chad put his arm around me, and I rested my head on his shoulder. He kissed my forehead, my nose, my lips.

"Mmm," I said.

"Happy?" he asked.

"Very."

A huge clap of thunder shook the car. Benedict let out a yip.

"Time to head for home." Chad kissed me once more, then started the car. The windshield wipers couldn't keep up with the torrent of water that cascaded out of the sky.

"Pull into the driveway," I said, when we reached my house. "It's closer."

"We're going to have to wait for this to let up. Even a short dash will get us soaked." We couldn't see out, the rain was coming down so hard.

There was a tap on the side window. Aunt Elise had braved the elements to bring us an umbrella. "Come inside!" she shouted when Chad opened the window a crack. "Hurry."

Chad went first, leaving Aunt Elise at the front door then returning with the umbrella. The street out front looked more like a river. He opened the door and half dragged, half carried Benedict to the house. I was last. We huddled together and ran.

"The power is out," Aunt Elise told us. "I have some candles in the cupboard."

"Do you have any games?" asked Chad.

"Clue," I said. "It's someplace in my closet. I'll try to find it."

The game was on my shelf, the lid of the box slightly dusty. It had been a long time since I'd taken it down. "The perfect game for a dark rainy afternoon." Chad gave a sinister laugh. "Do you really believe the butler did it, my dear?" He wiggled his eyebrows.

Benedict, who had taken refuge under the table, barked at him.

"See? Benedict knows you're guilty," I said, as we set up the game.

"Not me," said Chad. He looked under the table. "Honest, Benedict."

Benedict's tail thumped slightly.

"You play with us, Aunt Elise," I said.

"Oh, I don't know how," she replied. "I'll watch."

The sky had grown darker, and the candle threw flickering shadows across the game board.

"We'll show you how," I said. "It's been a long time since I've played, too, so I'll have to read the directions anyway."

"Very well."

We spent the rest of the afternoon playing Clue. Even though Aunt Elise insisted she didn't know how to play, she won almost every game. Outside, the rain had tapered off to a gentle but steady shower that threatened to go on forever.

Saturday's weather set the pattern for the next week. April showers had come in May. We trudged in and out of school with wet feet and drippy umbrellas.

We continued to work on the mural. On Thursday, Derrick and Chad painted the last strokes, while the rest of us watched and applauded. I felt happy, but sad, too. I knew that soon high school would be over. The days were racing by.

Then it was Friday. Chad drove me home from school.

"Do you think you'll be home in time for the

party tomorrow night?'' I asked.

"I'll try. That's all I can say. If the plane is on time and the traffic isn't too heavy, maybe. Go with Fred and Brita. I'll meet you there if I can." Chad pulled me into his arms and kissed me.

I clung to him. One day in Massachusetts seemed like forever. I felt like crying. It was silly, I told myself.

Then he was gone. I went inside. The house was empty. Aunt Elise had gone to sign up for her art class at the community center.

I let Benedict inside and hugged him. "Chad will be back for the party. I know he will," I said. What was wrong with me? I was acting as if this were the end of the world. One day without him and I was falling apart.

"I'd better pack my bag for tonight," I said. "Come keep me company, Benedict."

Always faithful and agreeable, Benedict followed at my heels.

"Be careful driving." My father handed me his car keys. "And be back by ten in the morning."

"Don't worry, Daddy." I kissed him and Aunt Elise, then patted Benedict. "I'll see all of you tomorrow."

Brita lived in a condominium with her mom and little brother. Her parents were divorced. Her mom worked as a legal secretary and was going to law school at night.

I pulled into their guest parking space, picked up my overnight case, then locked the car.

Brita was watching for me. She opened the door

before I could ring the bell, then grabbed my overnight case. "Come and see what I got to wear to Toni's party." She dragged me toward her bedroom.

Brita's room was painted white. Her spread, pillows, and curtains were a red, blue, yellow, and green-flowered print. The carpet was grass-green.

"What do you think?" She pulled a white jumpsuit with a turquoise belt from the closet.

"It's gorgeous," I said.

"And I got turquoise earrings to match. And two bracelets. Mom got a raise, so she was in a good mood when we went shopping."

"I don't know what I'm going to wear." I sat on the day bed, which had a trundle beneath. "With Chad gone, I can't seem to get enthusiastic."

"He might get back in time. You two are really serious, aren't you?" Brita hung her jumpsuit in the closet again and came to sit beside me.

"I guess we are. But so are you and Fred."

"You don't know how serious. We've been talking about getting married."

"Married! When? How?"

"Oh, I don't know. Nothing's definite at all. It's just talk. We can't really afford a wedding. Fred suggested that we just move in together while we're at college. Lots of kids do. Then when we graduate we could get married."

"Do you want to do that?"

Brita shrugged. "In a way it sounds wonderful. But, I don't know. It's such a big decision. Just as

big as whether or not to get married. Fred and I
have to talk some more.''

''What would your mother say? I know what
my dad and Aunt Elise would say.''

''My mother might not object. Fred and I have
been going together for two years now and she
knows how serious we are. And since marriage
didn't work out so well for her and my dad, I
think she'd think we were smart to try living
together before we actually got married. I don't
think she'd like me to move in with just any guy,
but Fred and I really love each other. I'm just not
sure. It's the biggest decision I've ever had to
make.''

''Are you . . . well, are you afraid of sleeping
with him?''

Brita smiled. ''Not afraid . . . but I don't think
I'm ready yet. This is one time when I can't jump
in impulsively. I still have a lot of growing to do,
Carolyn. I want to know who I am, where I'm
going, and what I have to offer before I make a
commitment. And there's more to consider than
sex, Carolyn. I'm not sure I'm ready for such an
intimate relationship. Being together all the time.
You know what I mean? Our clothes in the same
closet, eating breakfast together, finding out if he
leaves towels on the floor and if he talks in his
sleep. Those are some of the reasons to live together, but I'm not sure I want to know all that
about Fred yet. And what if I find out I don't like
him as much as I thought? We have a lot of fun
together. All of that might be spoiled. I guess I'm
not ready to get married or to live with someone.''

Brita sighed. "Sounds as if I've decided, but I haven't told Fred yet."

"Do you think Fred will be angry that you don't want to live with him?"

"If he is, then I'll know it wouldn't have worked. Maybe in a year I'll feel differently and be ready. I can always change my mind. If he really loves me, then he'll wait and he won't pressure me. So, tell me about you and Chad."

"I love him."

"I know that. What are your plans?"

"We don't have any. Isn't love enough for now?"

"Of course it is. You probably haven't even thought about getting married yet."

"I've thought about what it would be like, but Chad and I haven't talked about it. It's too soon for us, too, Brita. We both have other things to finish first."

"I guess that's it. There are other things to experience, other things to finish first, as you say. Once my mom said she envied us. She said when she was in high school, a lot of the girls were engaged. And if you didn't have a boyfriend, people thought you were weird. She said a lot of her friends got married because it was what you were supposed to do before you turned twenty-two. And a lot of those marriages fell apart. I just know I want my marriage to last forever."

"Me, too."

Brita jumped up. "Serious talking makes me hungry. Let's fix some pizza. Mom has class so she'll be late and my brother is staying at our dad's apartment for the weekend, so we can eat the whole thing ourselves. Listen. It's raining again.''

The gentle beat of rain sounded against the windows as I followed Brita down the hall to the kitchen. Was it raining in Massachusetts tonight, too?

❧ *Twelve* ❧

It was still drizzling when I left Brita's house the next morning. I drove slowly through flooded streets. Would the rain never stop? I wondered.

Aunt Elise had decided that this would be a good Saturday to clean the kitchen cupboards. I unpacked my overnight bag, then went to help her. Keeping busy helped pass the time quickly. I kept hoping the phone would ring and it would be Chad saying he'd gotten home much earlier than he'd expected. It didn't happen.

Fred and Brita were coming to pick me up at eight. I decided to wear a pale-pink sundress with a matching jacket. I fastened my shell necklace and wished that Chad were there. While I finished my makeup, I thought about the party and wondered if Toni's house would be large enough to hold all of us. What if she had been counting on nice weather so that everyone could go outside?

When Fred and Brita came to the door, Benedict followed close behind me. He whined and barked while we stood in the entryway talking with my father and Aunt Elise.

"What's the matter with him tonight?" asked my father.

"Maybe there's more thunder," I said.

"Or maybe he wants to go along," said Aunt Elise.

I patted Benedict on the head. "I'm not going to the park," I told him. "You have to stay here. Be a good puppy."

"It looks like the rain has stopped for a while," said my father, peering out the doorway. "I'll put Benedict in the backyard. Maybe if he stretches his legs, he'll feel better. This weather has kept him cooped up inside, too."

Benedict's tail began to wag as my father led him away.

"Have you heard from Chad?" Fred asked, as we walked down the front path to the car.

"No." I sighed. "I guess he's not going to get home in time for the party."

"You can still have fun," said Brita.

"Sure. I'll dance with you," offered Fred.

"Thanks. I'm still going to feel out of place."

"There will be other kids there without dates," said Brita. "Toni didn't make this a couples-only party. I heard Mr. Van Lawrence might even be there."

Their attempts to reassure me didn't help. I knew it was silly, but having Chad there seemed so important.

As we drove away from the front of the house, I heard Benedict barking in the yard. Maybe he did think we were going to the park. He hadn't been out for a walk in a while. It had been too wet.

Toni's street was lined with cars when we arrived. When I saw her house—modern white stucco, with roofs that slanted in several directions and lots of glass—I knew she didn't have to worry about the party being too crowded; there would be plenty of room. Inside, a beautiful woven rug hung on the entry wall. A glimpse into the living room at the left showed lots of glass-and-chrome furniture. The predominant color was white with accents of red and gray.

A Duran Duran album was playing on the stereo someplace against a background of talk and laughter.

"Welcome. I'm Lin Mai, Toni's mother," said a petite woman with dark hair pulled back in a smooth bun. She wore a red-and-white cotton dress and looked like her daughter. "The party is through the kitchen to the right, then straight ahead, then down the steps."

We didn't have trouble with her directions. Three steps down led us to a huge recreation room. The floor was all dark-blue ceramic tile. One whole wall was glass with sliding doors that went out onto a brick patio. The other walls were paneled in light wood. Some of the boys were playing pool at a table at the far end of the room. Just to the left of the stairs, a long table was covered with plates of food—everything from chips and dip to bowls of strawberries and plates of sandwiches. There was a bowl of punch and plenty of soft drinks.

"Come on in," called Toni. She ran to meet us. "I was hoping the patio would dry up a little more so we could spread out. But it doesn't look as if we'll be able to. Dance. Eat. Have fun." She turned to greet some other kids arriving behind us.

"We will have fun," Fred said. "Did either of you know she lived in a house like this?" he asked.

"No," I said.

"I did. Her father owns an import/export business," explained Brita. "Her mother is a textile artist. Did you see the rug in the entry? That's one of her works. Toni says she'll be famous one of these days."

"I think I'll go into import/export," Fred said. "I love this shack."

"I'd love some food," said Brita. "How about you, Carolyn?"

I wasn't very hungry. I'd had dinner just before we came, but I picked up a small plate and put a few strawberries and a sandwich on it. If I nibbled slowly, eating would pass the time.

Fred and Brita ate, too, then danced. The room was now comfortably crowded. I went over to watch the pool game. Derrick was also good with a pool cue. He and Mr. Van Lawrence were playing a game with plenty of bystanders offering comments and advice.

As I wandered from place to place, I kept imagining what it would be like if Chad were here. We could dance to the slow music that was playing, go out on the patio—even if it was wet—and see the gardens, just be together. I tried not to feel depressed, but it was difficult. Some of my old shyness seemed to be taking hold as I watched the others having fun. I sat down on the steps.

"Would you like to dance?" The question came from behind me.

"What?" I looked back. "Chad?" I must be dreaming, I thought. "Chad!"

"I promised I'd try to make it to the party, didn't I? Chad Bennington doesn't go back on his word."

"Oh, Chad, I missed you." I jumped up and threw my arms around him.

"The welcome was worth going away for a day," he teased. Then, more seriously, he said, "I missed you, too."

"You look tired." I brushed his hair back from his forehead. He had dark circles beneath his eyes.

"I am. We flew out late, then went straight to the college. And I didn't change my mind, but my parents had a good time. We visited some friends of theirs, so I didn't get much rest. And we got in only a while ago. I changed and came right here."

"Before we dance, are you hungry? There's lots to eat over there."

"Let's dance first." He held his arms out to me. "I want to hold you close," he whispered in my ear. "You can't imagine how much I missed you."

"Yes, I can," I said. "This has been the longest day ever. I didn't think you'd make it tonight."

"Well, I did." He kissed my cheek. "I love you," he whispered in my ear.

"I love you, too," I whispered back.

Someone changed the record to a rock album.

"Now let's get something to eat," said Chad. "I really am beat."

"We don't have to stay long," I said. "You should go home and get some sleep."

Fred and Brita came over to say hello.

"You look happy again, Carolyn," teased Fred. "I was beginning to think we'd have to put your chin in a sling, it was dragging so low."

Chad laughed and hugged me. "I don't think we'll stay long," he said.

"Uh-huh," said Brita. "A few hours apart, and they want to be alone."

"Maybe I should go away for a couple of days," Fred said.

"Don't you dare!" Brita put both arms around him. "I won't let you go."

"I should have tried that before," said Fred.

"Don't get too sure of yourself, mister," cautioned Brita. "I don't like that kind of game-playing."

Fred hugged her close. "What kind do you like, honey?"

"Tennis. Love or nothing," replied Brita.

"I don't think she's ever played tennis," Chad said, "but she has the right idea."

Toni came up to say hello to Chad. Everyone talked while I listened. I was just happy to have Chad back home.

"There's another slow song. One more dance, Carolyn, then we'll leave, if you don't mind."

"I don't mind," I said. "It's after eleven anyway."

Chad's car was parked way down the street. We walked slowly, with our arms around each other.

The air smelled fresh and overhead stars peeked through the scattered clouds.

"I think the rain is finally over," I said.

Chad yawned. "Excuse me. I think I need some sleep."

"Then let's go home."

At my house, we parked in front. Chad kissed me over and over until we were both breathless and my pulse raced. I snuggled close to him, not wanting to let go ever again.

"I think I missed you," he said.

"I know I missed you," I sighed. "I don't want to, but we'd better go inside."

"Mmm. You're probably right." He kissed me once more, then opened the car door.

Aunt Elise was still up when I stepped into the house. "Carolyn," she said, "is that you?"

"Come in for a minute, Chad," I said. "Yes, it is," I answered.

She came from the living room, a worried look on her face.

"You didn't have to wait up for me," I said. "Look who's back."

"Hello, Chad." She put a hand on my arm. "Benedict is gone."

"Benedict? But where? When? He was here when I left."

"I know and he carried on something awful. Your father said he could stay outside until he calmed down. When I went to let him in after he'd been quiet for a while, he was gone. I think he dug his way out of the yard."

"But he's never done that before," I said.

"He must have thought you were going to the park," said Aunt Elise. "He hasn't been out in a few days and he wanted to go. I'm sure he'll come back. I thought maybe he was with you," she finished in a tiny voice.

"He does know how to get to the park," I said.

"I'll drive down that way," offered Chad. "If I find him, I'll bring him back; otherwise I'll go home, and we'll look first thing in the morning. Don't worry. He's a big dog. And it's not going to rain tonight." Chad said good night and left.

"Oh, Benedict," I said, going to the window, "where are you?" I thought about him in the park in the dark, where the grass was wet and cold. He'd always slept on the soft, warm rug beside my bed.

An hour passed. Each time I heard a car, I ran to the door. I even called Benedict, but there was no answering bark.

"Go to bed, dear," said Aunt Elise, who had changed into her gown and robe. "You can look tomorrow. He might even be on the front doorstep in the morning."

Reluctantly I let her push me toward my room. I put my pajamas on, but couldn't seem to go to sleep.

It was one-thirty when the phone rang. I grabbed the receiver. "Hello?"

"Is this Carolyn?" asked a woman's voice.

"Yes." Who was calling at this hour? The voice wasn't at all familiar.

"This is Mary Bennington. Is Chad there?"

"Chad?" My heart leapt to my throat. "No.

Chad left over an hour ago.'' I sat up and switched on my bedside lamp.

"Are you sure, dear?"

"Yes. My dog ran away, and Chad said he would drive by the park and come back here if he found him, otherwise he'd go right home. He hasn't come back, so he should be there." What could have happened to Chad?

"Well, maybe he drove a little farther to look for your dog. If he comes back to your house, please have him call. We're very worried."

"Oh, I will. Mrs. Bennington, if he comes home, will you ask him to call me, just so I know he's all right?"

"Of course, dear."

"And call me again if he doesn't show up."

"Oh, I'm sure he'll be along soon."

"Yes. Yes, he will," I said. But neither of us sounded very convinced.

"Carolyn, who was that?" Aunt Elise and my father both stood in my bedroom doorway. I hadn't heard them come in.

"Chad's mother. He isn't home yet. Aunt Elise, he was so tired when he left. . . ." I stopped as I remembered what she'd told me about her fiancé. I shouldn't have said anything. "Chad is probably still out looking for Benedict. You know how he and that dog are. His parents are really upset because he's so late."

"I'll go and look," said my father. "Where was he going?"

"To the park," I said. "Can I come?"

"You stay here in case his parents call again."

Aunt Elise sat on the edge of my bed. She put her arms around me.

"I'm so worried," I said.

"I know, dear. I know." She rubbed my back, and I tried not to cry.

⇒§ *Thirteen* §⇐

"I can't just sit here." I paced to the window and back. My father's car started, and the headlight beams swept across the front of the house as he turned onto the street.

"Put your robe on, dear." Aunt Elise held out my bathrobe and I slipped my arms in. "Let's have some tea," she said.

"No. I couldn't eat or drink anything." I glanced at the phone, wishing it would ring and I'd hear Chad's voice. "I'm going to call his house. Maybe he's home now."

Aunt Elise came to stand beside me. "If he's not, tell his mother that Tom has gone to look for him. That may ease her mind."

I nodded. My fingers felt weak as I dialed the phone.

"Chad?"

He wasn't there: I knew from the way his mother had answered the phone.

"No. It's Carolyn, Mrs. Bennington. I was hoping . . ."

"He isn't home. Maybe we should call the police."

"The police! Do you think . . ." I couldn't finish my sentence. I wouldn't think anything terrible. Thinking terrible thoughts might make them come true. "My father has gone down to the park to look," I said.

"Chad's father is getting dressed now."

"His father is going to look for him, too," I told Aunt Elise.

"Let me," said Aunt Elise. She took the phone from my hand.

"Mrs. Bennington, this is Elise Dawson, Carolyn's aunt. Tell your husband to wait for a while before he goes out. We live only a few blocks from the park, so Tom should be back shortly. We'll call as soon as we know something. And if Chad shows up in the meantime, please let us know."

She nodded her head as Mrs. Bennington said something.

"That's a good idea," Aunt Elise responded. "We'll talk to you again in half an hour." She hung up.

"We're going to keep calling back and forth until we find out something. They're going to check the hospitals."

"The hospitals! You don't think that Chad— that something— Oh, Aunt Elise." I buried my face against her shoulder as the tears that couldn't be contained a minute longer burst forth.

I should never have asked him to come to the

party. It was my fault, all my fault. He was so tired. He should have stayed home. I should have stayed home. And Benedict? What had happened to Benedict?

"Shsh. Quiet, dear. Don't cry. Keep good thoughts. Tom will be back in a little while. Come into the kitchen. I know you said you weren't hungry or thirsty, but a little warm tea will make you feel better." With her arm around my shoulders, she guided me toward the kitchen.

"Maybe we should put the radio on." I pressed a tissue to my eyes, then blew my nose. "Maybe there's a traffic jam or something."

"If that will ease your mind, go right ahead."

My hand shook as I turned the dial on the small kitchen radio. Music. Only music. No news. No weather. Nothing. I turned it off. Right now I hated music. The happy chatter of the disc jockeys seemed to grate on my nerves. I went to the window and looked out. The street was dark, the other houses silent and shut down with sleep.

"Drink your tea," said Aunt Elise. She sat at the table, her hands wrapped around a fat, steaming mug.

I dropped onto the chair across from her. Was she remembering another time, another boy? I wondered. I wanted to reach out and comfort her, but my own pain seemed to form a shell around me.

I'm beat, Chad had said. *I promised I'd come. I love you.*

I picked up the mug and took a sip of tea I didn't even taste. I was only aware of the warmth slipping down my throat toward my churning stomach. Chad, where are you?

The phone rang. I jumped up. "Hello!"

"Has your father come back?" Mrs. Bennington sounded so tired.

"Not yet. No."

"He's not in any of the hospitals, thank God. We're going to call the police. Chad's father thinks they should be notified, so they can watch for him . . . for the—the car." Her voice broke, and my own tears welled up to burn behind my eyes again.

"I'll call you back the minute my dad gets here," I said. "I promise."

I hung up and went into the living room, where the window was large. I pulled the drape back and peered out, craning my neck to see as far down the street in the direction of the park as I could. I wanted to see a headlight. I wanted to hear Benedict bark. Most of all, I wanted to see Chad coming up our front walk.

I closed my eyes and pressed my forehead to the window. Nothing's happened, I thought. He's all right. His car had a flat tire or something. Nothing's happened. Nothing's happened. It's my imagination. I'm making things seem worse than they are. Just because Chad was so tired—just because Aunt Elise—just because . . . *Where was he?*

Tears were running down my face again, but I didn't try to stop them. I couldn't stop them.

The phone rang again, but I didn't run to answer it this time. A few minutes later, Aunt Elise came into the living room and turned a lamp on. "The police can't do anything for twenty-four hours," she said. "Mr. Bennington is getting ready to go out to look, too."

I didn't answer. I just looked out the window, staring as hard as I could through blurry eyes, seeing nothing but shadows in the dark, empty street.

I'll drive by the park, he'd said. But what if he went back to the party or stopped by Fred's house? Could he have done that? I ran to the phone in my room and dialed Brita's number.

"Hello?" Brita sounded sleepy, dazed.

"Brita, wake up. It's Carolyn."

"Who?"

"Carolyn. Brita, please wake up."

"Mmm. I am. What time is it? Carolyn, what do you want? What's wrong?"

"Have you seen Chad?"

"Chad? He was at the party. But you were there, too. Wait a minute while I turn a light on. I'm not awake."

The receiver banged; it sounded as if she said something to her mother, then she came back to the phone. "Why are you calling me about Chad?"

"He isn't home. Oh, Brita." I was crying again. What percent of the body is water? Why was I having such weird thoughts? I was tired, so tired. Chad had been tired, too.

"Maybe his car broke down someplace," said Brita.

"But why hasn't he called home?" I tried to get my tears under control. "He didn't come back to the party?"

"The party broke up right after you left. Do you think he might have gone to Fred's house? I'll call there and call you right back."

"Thanks. Hurry."

"Hey, don't worry. I'm sure he's all right."

"Sure. Call Fred, please." I hung up. He's all right, I thought. He is all right. He has to be all right. Why did I keep remembering what had happened to Aunt Elise's fiancé? Why couldn't I forget all about that? This wasn't the same. It couldn't be the same. I didn't want it to be the same.

The phone rang and I jumped. I grabbed the receiver.

"Fred hasn't seen him, either. He says he'll go out to look if you want him to."

"My dad is out and Chad's dad is going out. I'll call if they want Fred to help. Thanks, Brita."

"Do you want me to come over?"

"No. There's nothing you can do. Oh, Brita, I'm so scared."

"I know, but try not to worry. Everyone's late once in a while. Once Fred's car broke down out on the highway and he had to wait a long time before a police car came by. Then they had to radio for a tow truck because there weren't any phones around. He didn't get home until four in the morning. Everyone was frantic. It happens all the time, Carolyn. I'm sure he's fine. Call me when you hear something," she said.

"Sure." I hung up. She didn't know about Aunt Elise.

Glancing over to the empty rug that had always been Benedict's bed, I tried to picture them together. Both all right. Both safe. Both alive.

I pulled my legs up to my chest and rested my

head on my knees. I wouldn't sleep until I knew that Chad was all right. I couldn't. I was vaguely aware that I was crying again, that my pajama legs were getting wet from my tears. My heart seemed to weigh a thousand pounds. I hurt all over. I shut my eyes tightly. It happens all the time. Cars break down. It happens all the time. The park was only a few blocks away. Chad, I thought. Chad.

⤳§ *Fourteen* §⤳

A car door slammed. I jolted upright. My legs were stiff. What time was it? Then I heard voices and a dog barked.

"Chad?" I jumped from my bed and raced for the front door. There was no one there. I opened the door and looked out. One car. My dad's. I felt wide awake. Where was he? And what about Chad?

"Close the kitchen door," I heard Aunt Elise say. "I'll get Carolyn. She's been absolutely frantic. Chad, call your parents right away."

Chad! He was here. Feelings of relief surged through me.

I met Aunt Elise coming out of the kitchen. She was smiling as if it were Christmas morning and she'd received the best present in the world. This had been hard on her, too. "All here safe and sound," she said, "and only slightly the worse for wear."

"Worse? Is Chad hurt? Where's Benedict? What happened?"

"Come in the kitchen, but don't let Benedict into the main part of the house. You'll see what I mean by worse. It's nothing that soap and water can't cure."

My father was talking on the phone when I entered the kitchen. "It's no trouble," he said. "Considering the hour, I'm sure you'll agree it's best. We'll arrange for the car to be pulled out in the morning. I'll let you talk to Chad again."

Chad took the receiver. When he saw me he winked. "Honest, Mom. I'm all right. No, the car is all right, too."

The car? Had he been in an accident?

Then Benedict bounded up to me. I jumped back. He was caked with mud, but otherwise he seemed fine. His tail was in high gear.

"Benedict, back over here. Sit," commanded my father.

Benedict left a mud trail as he turned and went to sit near the back door.

I crossed the kitchen and sat down at the table with my father. "What happened?" I asked. "Where did you find them?"

"I'll let Chad tell you." He pushed his hair back from his face and yawned. "Elise, how about a glass of milk? Then I'm going to hit the hay for a few hours."

I glanced at the kitchen clock. It was almost three o'clock. It seemed as if it should be at least five.

"May I wash my hands?" asked Chad, after he'd hung up the phone.

"Your hands! Have you seen the rest of you?" Aunt Elise asked him. "Yes, wash your hands and

face, then sit down and have something to drink.
I'll get you a towel and Tom can give you some pajamas. You need a shower."

"Yes, ma'am," Chad said.

His appearance hadn't registered until now. He
looked almost as bad as Benedict, I realized. Mud
streaked his face. I noticed that his shoes were sitting on paper inside the back door and they looked
more like clay shoes than tennis shoes. He had
mud up to his knees and mud on his arms and
shirt.

"Did you fall in the mud?" I asked him.

My dad looked at me. He looked at Chad. Then
suddenly everyone was laughing.

"You might say that," said Chad, scrubbing
the mud off his hands and face. "But I'm not
hurt; and, listen, I don't have to stay here. I'll
drive home—" He stopped and looked chagrined.
"Oh, I forgot. No car. I guess I will stay here."

"Even if you had a car, you'd stay here," said
Aunt Elise. "I need some beauty sleep, in case you
haven't noticed."

"You could have fooled me," Chad replied.

"Flattery will get you a glass of milk and some
cookies, Mr. Bennington. Now tell us what happened," she said.

With glasses of milk all around and a plate of
cookies in the center of the table within everyone's
reach, Chad started from the time he left my
house to look for Benedict.

"I knew how worried you were about your dog,
Carolyn. We figured he might have headed for the
park. It wasn't a problem for me to swing by there
and check it out. So that's what I did.

"But when I drove into the parking lot, I didn't see any sign of Benedict."

Benedict moaned slightly and stretched out on the paper by the door. He always seemed to know when we were talking about him. He was also probably unhappy because he hadn't been offered a cookie.

"I was going to leave and go home and call you with the bad news. Then I realized that if he had gone to the park, he was probably someplace around the pond, where we always go to feed the ducks. So I drove to the edge of the parking lot and got out of the car to go see."

"And then the car wouldn't start again?" I asked.

"Let him tell us, honey," said Aunt Elise. She passed the cookies to me.

"As soon as I stepped out of the car, I knew I had a problem. The park at night is completely black. No lights at all. I couldn't even see the path. So I tried calling Benedict. It's really an odd feeling to be calling a dog in the middle of the night when it's pitch dark. I started out kind of softly, then got enough nerve to give a good shout. When I did that, I thought I heard him bark, but I couldn't see him. So I called again. And then I knew I heard him. But he didn't come. I tried walking a little but couldn't see where I was going."

"So what did you do?" I asked.

"I went back to the car to see if there was a flashlight in the glove compartment. There was, but the batteries were dead. So I thought that if I turned on the headlights, they might shine far enough to show me the way.''

"Then the car battery went dead?''

"No. Worse. The headlights had good strong beams, but they weren't pointed in the direction of the pond. So I backed the car up and pulled it at an angle, but while I was doing that I didn't notice that I was also driving off the pavement. And after all the rain we've had lately, the ground was soggy and the left front wheel sank into the mud.''

"All because of Benedict,'' I said.

"I should have watched what I was doing,'' said Chad. "Anyway, I tried to get the car out but the more I tried, the deeper I sank. Finally I gave up and went to find Benedict. The lights were aimed in the right direction. He was right by the park bench, but he'd gotten some fishing line or kite string—I'm not sure which it was in the dark—tangled around his leg and then around the bench leg. He had tied himself up and couldn't get free. There might even be some pieces tangled in his fur. He was really a mess—still is a mess.

"Of course, he was so glad to see me that he tried to jump on me and I fell over. Finally I got him calmed down and untangled then back to the car; but he didn't want to get in. When I managed to convince him to get in the backseat, I tried to dig the car out, but I didn't have a shovel or any tools except a tire jack, so it wasn't going too well. That's when your dad showed up. He tried to pull the car out, but it will take a tow truck to get it loose.''

"Why didn't you just walk back here?'' I asked.

"That's what I was planning to do next. I didn't

realize it was so late. I guess it took me longer to deal with the car and untangle Benedict than I thought. Working in the dark isn't so easy, you know.''

"Chad, I'm sorry," I said.

"No. I'm sorry. I didn't mean to worry everyone. My mom and dad sounded frantic when I called. And I've kept you up all night.''

"Brita! I promised her I'd call back." He'd reminded me that she was waiting for some word, too.

"Why do you have to call Brita?" asked Chad.

I explained how I'd wondered if he'd gone back to the party or to Fred's.

"Shouldn't you wait a couple of hours?" asked my father.

"No. She probably couldn't get back to sleep. I'll call her now. And Fred might be waiting to hear from her." I put my hand over Chad's. "I'm so glad you're all right.''

"I'm fine, Carolyn." He sandwiched my hand between his and smiled. Unspoken messages traveled between us.

I felt my father and Aunt Elise watching us. Tears welled up in my eyes, but I swallowed and got up in a hurry so no one could see them. Why was I going to cry now when everything was all right?

"Let me get you a towel, Chad. I'll make up the couch in the study. Don't anyone get up early," ordered Aunt Elise.

"Maybe I should take Benedict in the shower with me," Chad suggested.

"Oh, no. You'll get to give him a bath tomorrow—you and Carolyn,'' said my father.

''Oh, beep,'' Chad said.

Everyone laughed.

It was strange to be in my bed in my room and know that Chad was sleeping on the couch under the same roof. I wondered if he was thinking about me. I'd wanted to kiss him and hug him, but we'd never gotten time alone; and I'd felt self-conscious with Aunt Elise and my dad there. So we'd just said good night and squeezed hands.

The clock said ten o'clock when I opened my eyes. The smell of bacon frying and coffee brewing made my stomach growl. I stretched and stared up at my canopy. Chad's here, I remembered.

The sun was shining brightly. I pushed back my curtain and looked out. Not a sign of rain anywhere. Fat birds hopped on the front lawn, poking between the blades of grass in search of a tasty bug.

I washed and dressed, choosing my old jeans and sweat shirt. There was work to be done today.

Chad was already at the table. He was wearing last night's clothes, but obviously Aunt Elise hadn't taken her own advice but had been up early to do some laundry. There wasn't a sign of dirt on his shirt or pants. Only his tennis shoes, sitting by the door, were still caked with mud.

''Good morning,'' I said.

''Good morning. I see you're wearing your dog-washing clothes.''

''Absolutely. And as soon as you get the car out of the mud and go home to reassure your mom and dad that you're in one piece, I expect you to show up here wearing your dog-washing clothes, too."

"Does not compute. Does not compute," said Chad.

"It had better compute," Aunt Elise said, putting a plate of bacon and eggs in front of me. She handed Chad a platter of coffee cake. "Or we might have to get a new robot."

"A new robot! Aunt Elise, can't we just get the old one adjusted? With a little TLC, I can fix him."

"A little TLC, huh? Well, I won't stay around to watch," she said. "I have some homework to do. When your father gets up, make him an egg, over easy, Carolyn."

"Me?" I asked. "But I've never made an egg."

"Time for you to start. I've been neglecting your education, as well as mine." Then she was gone out of the kitchen.

Chad reached for a pencil on the counter. He scribbled something on his napkin, then got up from the table. He stopped behind my chair and bent over to kiss me.

"Ahem. Good morning."

We both jumped as my father entered the kitchen.

"Good morning, sir. I'd better call the tow truck," said Chad.

"I'll fix your egg, Daddy." I knew I was blushing.

"Stay where you are and finish your own breakfast, Carolyn. I'm in no hurry. I want to look at the paper. Chad, tell the garage to come in about an hour. I'll drive you over to the park." He poured himself a cup of coffee.

"Yes, sir." Chad dropped his napkin in my lap and went to the phone.

I picked up the napkin and unfolded it at the same time my father opened his paper. There were four words printed across the napkin: Beep! I love you.

Chad was talking on the phone. I held up the napkin. He smiled and winked. I smiled and winked back.

Across the table from me, my father turned the pages of his paper.

I'd take a chance on Chad anytime, I thought, as I sipped my coffee. I reached for another napkin to write a note back to Chad. Beep! I love you, too! I wrote.